Lamplight Tales

by

Roberta Simpson Brown

PublishAmerica
Baltimore

© 2004 by Roberta Simpson Brown.
All rights reserved. No part of this book may be reproduced, stored in a retrieval system or transmitted in any form or by any means without the prior written permission of the publishers, except by a reviewer who may quote brief passages in a review to be printed in a newspaper, magazine or journal.

First printing

At the specific preference of the author, PublishAmerica allowed this work to remain exactly as the author intended, verbatim, without editorial input.

ISBN: 1-4137-5524-0
PUBLISHED BY PUBLISHAMERICA, LLLP
www.publishamerica.com
Baltimore

Printed in the United States of America

Dedication

I dedicate this book to my extraordinary husband, Lonnie E. Brown, whose loving support and honest criticism makes my writing and storytelling possible.

And I also dedicate it to all my family and friends who have told me stories and listened to mine—especially my great-great nephews, Shawn and Steven, and my special friends, Sarah and Erin, who illustrate the meaning of *really great young people*!

Acknowledgments

My thanks to all the storytellers who made me aware of the value of storytelling and taught me the art.

I was born on my grandmother's farm in a time when life was not full of initials like PC, TV, VCR, VHS, CD, and DVD. It was a time in our culture when friends and families gathered at night and provided their own entertainment from imagination and personal experiences. This was a time when most people did not have electricity. While the moon slipped from cloud to cloud, shadows scurried to the corners of our rooms, held back only by the light from oil lamps. These shadows seemed to come alive as we shared our spooky stories, so we inched closer to each other to face our fears together as we listened.

Times have changed now, but scary stories have endured. As a professional storyteller, I specialize in telling these frightening lamplight tales to all types of audiences across the country. They still entertain and thrill us. They still help us deal with our fears by sharing our experiences. They continue to be one of the oldest art forms of our culture that brings us together.

Thanks to all of you who pass the stories on and keep the tradition alive.

Contents

To Bear Arms 7
Neighborhood Watch 12
Ghost Chains 16
The Christmas Tree 19
The Little White Calf 22
Snow Angel 27
Toe Jam 29
The Touch 33
Homeward Bound 36
The Haunting of Damron's Creek 40
The Boundary Oak 43
Crying in the Rain 48
He'll Come Knocking 51
Night Walkers 56
Draculanterns 62
Fishing Creek Hill 64
The Woman at the Spring 67
Wildcat Cave 69
Pool Parties 73
Hauntspitality 76
The Pine Thicket 80
The One That Got Away 83
Searchers 86
Wings 90
Horse Calls 95
Crawl Space 99
Family Recipe 102
Hearing Loss 106

To Bear Arms

It was a night of the hook moon when Ben Jackson woke up from a fretful sleep. The hook moon was supposed to have the power to pull the restless dead from their graves, so he thought that maybe it had pulled him from a restless sleep. He listened to see if he could hear a more realistic explanation for waking in the middle of the night. He didn't have to listen long before he heard it. Something was moving along the edge of the woods near the farmhouse.

Ben got up and crossed to the open window. The sliver of moon gave little light, but Ben could see that threatening dark clouds had built into a massive bank beyond the creek. A flash of lightning exposed a huge, shadowy form for an instant before it disappeared among the trees.

"It can't be a bear," he said to himself. "I killed the only one around here last week."

As if to confirm it, he looked at the sun porch where he'd spread the bear skin out to dry. The bear's head was caught by the pale moonbeams, which glittered in its eyes and gave them the look of a living, breathing thing. Ben imagined they were focused on him, and he stood there feeling uneasy, even a little afraid.

Fear was something Ben Jackson did not often experience. Everybody said he was the best hunter in the county and he wouldn't hesitate to take on anything. Tonight brought a different feeling, though. He knew it was crazy, but he felt like something was stalking him tonight—something that was not of this world. He fought the urge to lock the window and hurry back to bed. He couldn't force his eyes from the tree line where the thing had vanished. Nothing was stirring now.

He had just about convinced himself that he had imagined the whole thing when he heard it moving again. A low growl came from the woods near the spot where he had shot the bear.

"It can't be another bear," he said out loud. "It must be thunder."

"What?" asked his wife, propping on one elbow in bed and rubbing the sleep from her eyes with the other hand. "What are you doing up at this hour?"

"I thought I heard thunder," said Ben. "I'm closing the window so the rain won't blow in. Go back to sleep."

He was relieved to find a logical excuse to close it. He didn't want to mention the dark form and the growling to his wife. She didn't approve of his hunting, and he didn't want to hear her opinion in the middle of the night, especially when there was something out there that he couldn't explain. He made sure the window was locked and then slid quickly into bed.

Ben lay very still so his wife could sleep, but it was an effort to keep from trembling. He heard something moving closer to the house, but he told himself it was just the wind. He heard the growling again as the black clouds crossed the moon, but he did not get out of bed to investigate. When the storm broke, the thunder and lightning sent a chill through his body like he'd never felt before. He surprised himself by inching closer to his wife's warm back beneath the covers. Her steady breathing gave him a small measure of comfort, and he allowed the patter of rain on the roof to lull him off to sleep.

He awoke to sunshine and the smell of breakfast. The new day made last night's events seem like a bad dream. He dressed and joined his wife in the kitchen. He gobbled his food and hurried to the barn to milk the cows.

As he carried the milk to the house, he crossed the sun porch and glanced down at the bearskin. He stopped short, his heart pounding. There was no doubt about it. The bearskin was now positioned closer to the window. He willed himself to be calm.

"The wind blew it there during the storm last night," he told himself. "There is nothing sinister about it."

He hadn't convinced himself, though. He knew he should move it back to the edge of the porch where it could get the morning sun, but he couldn't bear to touch it.

He looked away and hurried inside.

He left the buckets of milk on the table for his wife to strain and store in the refrigerator. He poured himself a second cup of coffee and sat at the kitchen table trying to figure out what was going on. He felt that the eyes of the bearskin were set on him from the doorway, but he refused to turn and acknowledge what he felt. He finally came to the conclusion that some kind of strange, large animal must be roaming the woods. The sensible thing to do was to go check it out.

Summoning his courage, he went to the rack beside the door and took his gun down. Then he took a deep breath and headed toward the woods.

"Where are you going with that gun at this hour, Ben Jackson?" his wife called.

"I thought I saw fox tracks near the chicken coups," he lied. "I'm going to check it out."

"Humph!" his wife grunted in reply, but at least she didn't give him her usual lecture. He didn't wait for her to change her mind.

The ground was wet and soft after last night's rain. Ben expected to find tracks that would explain the sound he had heard before the storm. He was surprised to find the ground undisturbed. Not a leaf had been moved, and oddly enough, not a leaf was moving now.

Ben's eyes searched the trees for a sign of life, but nothing stirred. These were danger signs, for sure. He gripped his gun tighter as the bushes began to rustle beside the path. Slowly, a huge shadow emerged in front of him. He strained his eyes to see what was casting the shadow, but nothing was there! Filled with panic, he whirled and fled headlong down the path toward home. Once he'd cleared the woods, he forced himself to stop to catch his breath. Thank God, nothing had followed him.

He looked around to see if anyone had been watching. He would be embarrassed if anyone had seen him running from a shadow in the woods like a scared rabbit. He'd never be able to explain why because he didn't even understand it himself. He had never been afraid of anything before. He had tracked that last bear, turned it toward his barn, and shot it in cold blood. He'd seen the pure hate and rage in its eyes as it fell, but that hadn't scared him. What a trophy it was for his collection! His neighbors had already been over several times to admire the bearskin.

As his breathing slowed after his mad dash from the woods, Ben looked back to make sure nothing was coming after him. A gentle breeze was moving the trees slightly now, and birds were flying serenely among the branches. Whatever had been there was gone. Ben took his gun inside and placed it back in the rack. Then he went about his work as usual. It was sun set before he had made up the lost time with his chores.

Ben was glad his wife had prepared an early supper. He excused himself from the table as soon as he swallowed the last bite.

"I'm exhausted," he told his wife. "I think I'll go on to bed. That storm kept me awake last night."

"Go ahead," she answered. "I have some sewing to catch up on. I'll be along when I finish."

Ben fell into a sound sleep as soon as his head touched the pillow. Hid dreams were disturbing, though. He dreamed he was inside a bearskin, walking through woods filled with hunters. Bullets zinged around his head until he woke up in a cold sweat.

He could hear the low hum of his wife's sewing machine. The sound was comforting. He closed his eyes and tried to sleep again, but a loud bump on the sun porch brought him to a sitting position. He held his breath and listened. Something was definitely moving out there. It wasn't his wife. She was still in her sewing room.

Ben slipped from beneath the covers and crept to the window. It was dark now, and the moon was no help with light. Another storm front must be moving through. He felt along the wall for the light switch. One flip and the sun porch was flooded by the light from the 100 watt bulb. He stood only a second, his eyes adjusting to the light, before a scream tore from his throat.

What he was looking at defied description. It was a massive, skinless thing, oozing blood from its bare muscles as it reached for the bearskin. Ben's scream drew its attention, and its bloody paw smashed through the window, grabbing Ben and pulling him outside. Ben's screaming continued.

His wife came running from her sewing as soon as she heard the commotion start. She reached the bedroom window in time to look out and see the bloody beast dragging Ben toward the woods.

She raced to the neighbors' house, babbling out of her mind. By the time they understood what had happened, they could find no trace of Ben Jackson. His wife burned the bearskin as soon as she was able to return home.

Nobody hunts in the woods or on Ben's farm anymore, unless it's old Bloody Bear looking for his skin!

Neighborhood Watch

When Granny Redmon's husband died, she stayed on alone in their cabin way out in the country.

"Move into town, Granny," people urged. "It's too dangerous to live out here alone."

"I'm not afraid," she'd tell them. "I've got my good neighbors, Wallace and Lily Mae, and little Walter. They watch out for my welfare and keep me company if I get lonely."

People finally gave up and let Granny have her way.

Granny and the Kells often visited each other after supper to talk until bedtime. All the Kells loved to hear Granny tell stories. When she told the scary ones, little Walter would bury himself beneath layers of quilts to keep the spooks away! Granny would laugh and walk home by herself.

One night Granny went to visit the Kells and stayed a little longer than she intended to. Clouds had moved in, and the moon that usually lit Granny's way was hidden. Granny hesitated at the door, wishing she had thought to bring her lantern.

"Take this lamp," said Lily Mae. "It belonged to my grandmother. If she were alive, I'm sure she'd be happy that somebody could get some good out of it."

Lily Mae lit the lamp and handed it to Granny Redmon. The globe was yellow and glowed like a Christmas light. It was the prettiest lamp Granny had ever seen.

"I couldn't take anything that's been in your family for generations," Granny protested. "What if I dropped it?"

"You won't," said Lily Mae. "Besides, I want you to keep it. Then if you ever need us for anything, just light this lamp and put it in the window. We'll see that it's a different color from your other lamps and know something is wrong. Then we can hurry over to help you."

Reluctantly, Granny thanked them and left with the lamp. The Kells watched the yellow light move through the darkness.

When Granny Redmon got home, she realized that the oil had burned up in the lamp. There had been just enough in it to get her home safely. It was too late to fill it up, so she put it aside and went to bed. In the days that followed, she forgot about the oil, so the lamp stayed empty.

One night, several weeks after the Kells had given her the lamp, Granny woke to see a light flickering through her window. At first she thought she was dreaming, and then wondered if she had not blown out her lamp when she went to bed. She sat up and saw that no lamps inside her house were burning. The light was coming from outside.

Granny looked out her window and was horrified to see that the Kells' house was engulfed in flames! She pulled on her clothes and hurried as fast as she could, calling out their names. Other neighbors had seen the flames and arrived about the same time, but there was nothing they could do.

The fire raged out of control and the heat was searing. Everyone watching the billowing smoke knew that nobody could have survived inside the inferno. Granny stood sobbing until someone led her back to her cabin and helped her to bed. She lay until daybreak staring at the lamp Lily Mae had given her. She would miss them all so much!

When the fire cooled down, Granny cried again as she watched their charred bodies being removed and carried away.

Time passed slowly, and Granny tried not to look at the skeletal remains of the house where her dear friends had lived. But each day she did. And each night, she felt a little less safe without them there.

Then came the winter day when nobody in the whole countryside felt safe.

Granny had started supper in the late afternoon when Wade Able knocked at her door to tell her the news. Old Aunt Jewell Dixon, who lived down the road from Able's store, had been robbed and stabbed to death.

Granny began to tremble, and Mr. Able helped her to a chair.

"Who would do such a horrible thing to such a sweet woman?" she asked him.

"A stranger stopped at my store about noon for a bologna sandwich and an RC Cola. He said he was a relative of Mrs. Dixon, and he asked a lot of questions about her.

When he went on his way, I began to get the feeling that there was something just not right about him. I called the sheriff and we went straight to her house. It was too late, though. She was dead and the stranger was gone."

"Do you think he's still in the area?" asked Granny.

"We're almost sure of it. That's why the sheriff and I are out warning people." replied Mr. Able. "Just stay inside and keep your door barred until we catch him. I'll come back or send someone you know to tell you. Don't open the door for anybody you don't know."

When Mr. Able left, Granny took his advice and barred the doors and windows.

"I don't have to worry," she thought. "Nobody would want anything I've got."

She tried to put it out of her mind, but every little sound made her jumpy. She went to bed early and fell asleep right away. She woke to see moonlight streaming through her window. Slowly, she realized that something was wrong. The window was open and someone was standing at the foot of her bed. A knife blade glittered in the moonlight.

Granny was paralyzed with fear. She had locked the window before she went to bed, but the lock was old. He must have broken it to get inside.

"Dear Lord," she prayed, "help me somehow!"

As she uttered the prayer, the lamp the Kells had given her flickered on the table near her bed. The golden light glowed against the window. For an instant, she was as startled by that as she was by the intruder. He must have been startled, too, because he stepped back into the shadows. It was then that Granny heard the voices outside—the voices of a man, woman, and child.

Granny and the intruder watched three shadowy forms float through the window by the lamp and stop between the man and Granny. They pointed accusing fingers at the man cringing in the corner as screams tore from his throat.

"Oh, Lord!" Granny thought. "Could this man have come through earlier and burned the Kells' home?"

Still screaming, the intruder dashed wildly to the window and leaped out. Granny heard one last shriek, and then silence as he fell on his knife.

Granny tried to move as she saw the three shadowy figures begin to turn toward her to make sure she was all right. Oh, God! She didn't want to see! She knew who they were before she saw the charred faces. It was the only time in her life that Granny Redmon ever fainted!

She revived to the sight of the sheriff and Wade Able bending over her. The lamp with the yellow globe was dark now that it had done its job.

Granny lived several more years after that night and died peacefully in her sleep. The yellow lamp was always her most prized possession, but it disappeared at her death.

Her old cabin is gone now, too, but some folks swear that they have sometimes seen a warm yellow light moving between the blackened foundation of the old Kell place and the spot where Granny's once stood. And they say that, if you listen hard on a moonless night, you can hear those neighbors' voices carried on the wind, still watching out for each other.

Ghost Chains

Ken Davis sat in the shadows studying the campers seated around the campfire. A little wimpy boy had been moved closer to the counselors, and two bullies had been separated in the circle. One of the counselors was getting ready to tell stories. Ken wondered if he would tell why the camp had been closed for four years.

Ken thought of that last camping session when he had been one of the campers. He could still hear the chains rattling tonight. The others campers must have heard something, too, because they glanced over their shoulders at the river. A jingle Ken had written flashed through his mind:

Ghost chains rattling,
Clank, clank, clank!
Splashing in the river,
Climbing up the bank,
Creeping 'cross the campground,
Circling the tent!
Death is in the air tonight!
I can smell the scent!

Ken listened with the others as the counselor began to speak. He reminded all the campers that they couldn't pick on each other. Ken was glad to hear that, because he could still remember how it had hurt him when they called him Skinny Kenny! He'd have to let these bullies know that they couldn't behave like that now, but he'd do it later after they had left the campfire circle. For now, he was content to hear the stories with the others.

The counselor told the story exactly as Ken remembered it. Four years ago, two bullies had played a deadly prank on a scrawny little camper. They had grabbed him, hauled him into a boat, and rowed to a small island in the river. They had taken a chain that had been left in the boat for docking, and they had chained the terrified boy to a tree.

Then they had rowed back to camp. They swore later that they had intended to go back for the boy after about half an hour, and Ken thought that was probably true, but a sudden storm dropped inches of rain on the camp without warning. A flash flood swept down the river, covering the island and drowning the boy chained to the tree.

When things had calmed down that night and parents had been notified that the campers would be sent home the next morning because of the tragedy, everybody went to their tents to try to sleep. It was then that a strange sound came from the river, and Ken thought of his jingle:

Ghost chains rattling,
Clank, clank, clank!
Splashing in the river,
Climbing up the bank,
Creeping 'cross the campground.
Circling the tent!
Death is in the air tonight!
I can smell the scent!

Suddenly screams from the tent shared by the bullies cut through the darkness. They stopped abruptly as the counselors rushed to see what was wrong. A puddle of river water stood pooled between the sleeping bags, and both boys lay dead from chain marks on their throats.

The camp closed after that night. Ken had to admit that he missed it. He was glad when new owners remodeled it and relocated campsites before reopening it this year. It was good to see campers back again.

Ken listened as the counselor ended his storytelling and sent the campers off to bed. He watched the fire die down, and heard the bullies teasing the little wimpy boy in their tent. Now was a good time to teach them a lesson.

Ken headed for the river. He had to get the chain from his watery grave before he made his rounds tonight. He smiled as he hummed his jingle:

Ghost chains rattling,
Clank, clank, clank!
Splashing in the river,
Climbing up the bank,
Creeping 'cross the campground
Circling the tent!
Death is in the air tonight!
I can smell the scent!

The Christmas Tree

It was Christmas Eve, a night for miracles, but Ellen Dixon felt there were no miracles left. For her, there was only grief. The flu epidemic that had hit the hill country of Kentucky, sometimes wiping out entire families, had spared her and her little daughter, Polly. Her husband Will hadn't been so lucky, though. On this Christmas Eve, he was lying under the snow down the road in the small graveyard by Bethlehem Church. It was going to be a bleak Christmas without him.

Still weak from the flu's devastating effects, Ellen lay on her bed watching Polly. The young girl was standing by the window, staring at the first heavy snowstorm of the season raging outside.

"Come on to bed and rest a while," said Ellen. "I don't want you to get sick again."

Polly didn't move.

"Polly, did you hear me?" her mother asked.

"Yes, Momma," Polly answered. "I'll be there in a minute. I'm waiting for Daddy to bring us our Christmas tree."

"Polly," Ellen said, her voice breaking like her heart. "You know that's not going to happen."

"But Daddy always gets us a tree," Polly argued. "He has every year of my life. I know he will remember."

"But he can't this year, Polly," Ellen tried to explain. "Daddy died, and he won't be coming back. I've been too sick to get a tree. You know that."

"But we've got to have a tree!" Polly insisted. "If we don't, how will Santa find us? How will he know where to put the presents?"

"Santa won't expect us to get a tree in this blizzard!" Ellen assured her. "I don't think even Santa will be out on a night like this."

"Santa likes snow," said Polly. "He'll want us to have our presents on Christmas morning!"

"Our presents will be late this year," Ellen told her. "I'm sorry. That's just the way it is! Now, come rest a bit, and I'll get up and fix us something for supper."

Reluctantly, Polly turned from the window and started toward the bed. Suddenly, a thud sounded on the front porch. Polly ran back to the window and looked outside.

"Momma, somebody is moving out there!" said Polly. "He's put something on our porch! Oh, Momma, look! It's a tree!"

"The wind must have blown a tree down," said Ellen. "There's nobody out in this storm!"

Ellen pulled the quilt around her and sat on the side of the bed. Polly ran to the door and jerked it open before Ellen could stop her.

"Polly! Close that door right now!" Ellen ordered.

Polly was too excited to hear her.

"Look, Momma!" she exclaimed. "Isn't it wonderful? Daddy brought us a tree after all!"

Polly began to tug at the tree, as Ellen struggled to her feet and hurried as fast as she could to the door.

"Help me pull it inside," said Polly.

Ellen used most of her strength to help pull the tree through the door. She closed the door quickly and turned to Polly, who was gazing raptly at the pine.

"I tell you, you're going to catch your death of cold or have a backset with the flu!" warned Ellen.

Polly grabbed a dishtowel and began to clean up the snow that had fallen to the floor from the branches.

"I told you Daddy would bring a tree!" she said.

"It was the wind," Ellen tried to explain. "The tree blew down in the storm."

"No, it didn't!" Polly persisted. "Look! It's been cut!"

Ellen looked at the trunk and saw that Polly was right. She searched her mind for an explanation.

"Some neighbor must have brought it," she said finally. "We'll have to find out who it was and thank them."

"Daddy brought it," Polly repeated. "I know he did!"

"But Polly——"Ellen interrupted.

Polly stopped and looked up at her mother.

"I know Daddy's dead, Momma," she said in a very serious voice. "But do you remember the story he used to tell me about Christmas Eve? He said it was a special time when animals could talk and the dead could walk about without leaving any tracks?"

"Yes," said Ellen. "I remember."

"Well, there were no tracks in the snow! I looked!" said Polly. "A neighbor would have left tracks. Daddy wouldn't!"

"Polly," Ellen tried to explain, "Daddy was just telling you a story. That's a blowing snow out there. It covered the tracks of whoever brought that tree."

She saw that Polly wasn't listening. She had gone to the closet and was looking inside for the tree stand and decorations.

"Momma," she called, "can you help me with the boxes?"

Ellen helped her lift the boxes from the shelf. The decorations were there, but the tree stand was missing.

"I think your father used to keep it in back of the closet on the floor," Ellen told her daughter.

The two of them looked down, as Polly tugged her mother's arm.

"Look at Daddy's shoes!" said Polly

Ellen saw the shoes just where Will had left them before he died. They were side by side inside the closet, only now they were covered with snow.

The Little White Calf

Virgil Dean stood looking at the bleak landscape that had once been his thriving farm. The Civil War had changed the good life he'd had with his family to one of devastating loss. The Rebels had come through Kentucky, burning many of the homes in their path. His had been one of them. He had thought of trying to rebuild, but he and his wife decided the place had too many sad memories.

Virgil had been forced to leave his family to fight for the Union, but he'd had the foresight to hide some money and other valuables in a small cave on their property. When the word came to Virgil's wife that the rebels were headed to the farm, she took their two children and hid undetected in the cave. When she and the children had finally been able to come out of hiding, they found the house burned and the farm animals slaughtered. They lived with relatives until Virgil came home. That's when they decided to start over in a new place. Virgil took one last look, loaded up his family, and moved on.

They traveled through two counties, looking for a farm they could afford with what they had hidden away. They met with one disappointment after another until they came upon a small farm one day that was for sale at a very low price. It even had a two-room log house, with a big boxed room in back.

Virgil moved his family in right away. They all agreed that the boxed room would be perfect for the children.

Virgil was a strict father, and even on the first night in their new home, he sent the children to bed early. About thirty minutes later, Virgil and his wife were getting ready for bed themselves when the two children came running in from the boxed room.

"What are you doing up?" Virgil demanded to know.

"We can't sleep," they told him. "The little white calf takes up all the room and we can't breathe."

"There's no calf in your room. You were just dreaming. Now get back to bed," Virgil ordered.

The children looked frightened, but they obeyed their father and returned to their room. Virgil and his wife turned in for the night a few minutes later and went right off to sleep.

Several hours passed, and suddenly Virgil woke up. At first he was confused about where he was. As his mind cleared from sleep and his eyes adjusted to the dark room, he saw two figures huddled by the fireplace. He realized it was the children and that they had awakened him while poking at the fire. He couldn't imagine why they were up. They knew better than to defy him when he told them to do something. Yet there they were, defiantly out of bed in the middle of the night, even though they knew they'd be punished.

Virgil sat up in bed and asked sternly, "Didn't I tell you two to go to bed?"

"Yes, Sir." they both answered

"Then why are you in here?" he demanded to know.

The older child explained, "It's the little calf, Daddy. It fills up the room and scares us."

"I told you before that there is no calf in your room," said Virgil. "Now get back to bed before I take a switch to both of you!"

Usually the threat of a whipping sent the children scurrying off to do as they were told, but they didn't move from the fireplace!

By now, Virgil's wife was awake and just as amazed as Virgil that the children were not obeying a direct order from their father. She knew they were scared when he threatened to whip them, but she could see that they were more afraid of facing that room than facing the switch!

"Wait a minute, Virgil," she said. "Maybe something got in that room that we didn't see. Children, where did the little calf come from?"

"The corner," said the younger child. "It started as a little ball of white light."

The older child nodded and added, "Then it grew and grew to the shape of a little white calf and filled the room. It took our breath away."

Virgil got up, crossed to the boxed room, and looked around. "There's nothing in here now, so stop this foolishness and go back to bed!"

Trembling, the children stood up and ran to their mother.

"Virgil, let's let them sleep by the fireplace in here tonight. Then tomorrow, we can check out the room," she suggested.

Virgil wasn't too happy with the idea, but he agreed in order to get some sleep.

In the light of morning, Virgil and his wife looked all around the room. There was nothing there that remotely resembled a calf.

"I think they were scared from being in a new place," he said. "I'm not going to have any nonsense about them sleeping in there tonight."

The children overheard their father and they knew he meant it. Their mother saw the dread in their eyes as the afternoon wore on. Then something happened to give them a temporary reprieve.

In the late afternoon, dark clouds began to bank up beyond the hills. With the beginning rumbles of thunder, a knock came at the door. A traveling salesman stood there, trying to sell wares. Salesmen were welcome in those days because families didn't get much company in rural areas and stores were usually far away. Virgil and his wife bought a few things they needed, and since the storm broke before they finished their business, they invited the man to stay for supper. When supper ended, the storm didn't, so Virgil told the salesman he was welcome to stay all night. The logical place to put him was in the boxed room, so the children happily made themselves a pallet by the fire.

All was peaceful during the first part of the night. The family and their guest went to sleep to the soothing sound of the rain falling on the roof. Then, during the pre-dawn hours, something woke Virgil. He opened his eyes to see a figure moving from the boxed room to the fireplace.

"What's the matter?" Virgil called out.

The salesman stood there, fully dressed and shaking.

"You'll think I'm crazy if I tell you," the man answered.

"I think you'd better tell us anyway," said Virgil.

Everybody else was awake now and listening.

"Well," said the salesman, "I slept fine at first. Then I woke up cold. I had plenty of cover, but the room had a damp chill. Over in the corner, a pinpoint of light appeared. It grew into a glowing white ball of light and then changed into a calf. It got bigger and bigger until it filled the room. I couldn't get any air to breathe, so I jumped into my clothes and got out of there as fast as I could. I think it disappeared as I went through the door."

"See, Daddy!" said the younger child.

"Now do you believe us?" asked the older.

"I believe you all saw something," Virgil admitted, "but I think there must be some sensible explanation. We'll have some breakfast and then check the room."

"No, thank you," said the salesman. "I wouldn't go back into that room for anything!" And he left without anything to eat.

Virgil had heard enough to be convinced that he shouldn't force the children to sleep in the room, but he made up his mind to find out what was going on. That night, he told the children to sleep in the room with their mother. Then he went to bed alone in the boxed room. Sometime after midnight, he woke his whole family as he came running out.

"It's just like you said," he told the children. "One way or another, I'm going to get to the bottom of this."

After breakfast, Virgil went to see the man who has sold them the farm.

"I think there may be something about our house that you failed to tell me," he told the man. "I'd like to hear the story about the boxed room."

"I'm sorry," the man sighed. "I thought maybe it wouldn't bother you. The farm belonged to my brother and his family. My nephew had a pet calf that he'd cared for from the day it was born. Food became scarce during the war, and when my brother couldn't get food anywhere else, he butchered the little white calf for food."

"Oh, Lord," said Virgil.

The man nodded as he continued.

"My nephew was heart broken. He refused to eat a bite of it. My brother was not a patient man. The boy didn't understand and my brother told him he was acting foolish. He forced the boy to eat some of his butchered pet. The boy became hysterical, but his mother got him to lie down in the boxed room. He immediately became violently ill and began vomiting. After midnight, he finally dozed off. Then a little later, his mother thought she heard him say 'You're here!' She thought he was only talking in his sleep, so she didn't get up to check on him. The next morning, she found him dead. After that, nobody could sleep in that room. My brother and his wife sold me the farm and moved across the country. I thought it was a family thing or I would have warned you."

Virgil thanked the man for telling him the story. He went home and built another room for the children on the other side of the house. Nobody ever slept in the haunted boxed room again. And if the little white calf came every night after that looking for the boy, nobody ever knew.

Snow Angel

When Miss Mandy got her first teaching job years ago, there were no hotels out in the country. It was the custom then to take a room with somebody in the community, so Miss Mandy rented a room in the home of Mrs. Sullivan, who made her living by taking in boarders after her husband died.

Miss Mandy's room was on the first floor by the front hall entrance, so she could clearly hear anyone coming and going through the front door. In fact, she often answered the door when visitors came so Mrs. Sullivan would not have to come downstairs if she was busy on the second floor.

One Saturday night, a deep snow fell and total quiet settled over the hills around the house. Miss Mandy could see the nearest neighbor's light twinkling far in the distance. Nothing was moving in between to break the crisp covering of white. It was a perfect night for staying inside a warm, cozy house, and that was exactly what Miss Mandy was doing.

She had finished grading a stack of papers and had started a book she'd been wanting to read, when she heard the outside door open into the front hallway. She thought it was one of the other boarders coming in, so she didn't think it was odd when she heard heavy footsteps stomping outside her door. She assumed someone had been for a walk and was trying to dislodge the snow from their shoes so they wouldn't track it through the house.

As she turned a page in her book, she heard heavy breathing and gasping from the hallway. She started toward the door to see if someone had become ill, but the heavy breathing stopped and the footsteps went back out the door.

She ran to her window to see who it was, but nobody was there. She looked in both directions, but nobody was in sight. She was amazed that there were no tracks among the freshly fallen flakes. She wondered if someone had collapsed by the door out of her view.

She hurried back to the door and opened it. There were no puddles of melted snow on the floor, nor was there a body. She stood there, completely puzzled.

"You heard him, too, didn't you?" she heard a voice say from the second floor landing.

She looked up to see Mrs. Sullivan looking down at her.

"Yes," she admitted. "Who was that?"

"I call him the Snow Angel," Mrs. Sullivan said, smiling.

"You know him?" Miss Mandy asked.

"He was around for a while before my husband died," she replied. "He used to live in the city, but he came to stay with some cousins over the ridge when his wife passed away. He wasn't happy there, though. There was nothing to do to take the place of the city activity he missed."

"I guess it would be hard to adjust," said Miss Mandy.

"Yes," continued Mrs. Sullivan, "it was hard. When it would snow, he'd get restless and walk across the ridge. He would come by and check on all of us to see if we needed anything. We used to invite him in for a hot meal or something to drink while he got warm by the fire. Then the flu hit and took lots of people here, including my husband. Our Snow Angel got sick, too, and his cousins wouldn't let him out in the cold."

"I'm surprised that they let him out tonight in this weather," said Miss Mandy.

"They can't help it," Mrs. Sullivan answered. "Whenever the snow comes now, he always checks on those of us who were kind to him."

"Do you think we should go look for him?" Miss Mandy asked. "He seemed ill. He might need some help."

"He needs nothing from us," Mrs. Sullivan assured her. "Why do you think I call him the Snow Angel? He fell and froze to death in a snowstorm several years ago."

Toe Jam

Nurse Tasha Hankins hesitated outside the door to the room in the nursing home where the old man had died. It was her first night back from vacation and it would be her first time to see the empty bed since the old man's death. She stood remembering him, afraid to go into the room because of a vague, gnawing feeling of guilt.

She hadn't actually been there when he'd died. That had happened a little over twenty-four hours after she had gone off duty. She assured herself that she had no reason to feel guilty, and she ignored the little twinges of conscience that said she did.

She vividly remembered the day she had seen the old man for the last time.

"I want some water," he'd said.

She had hurriedly poured him some from the pitcher by his bed, even though she knew the water would be lukewarm. She hadn't wanted to take the time to fill the pitcher with ice just then. She'd been in a hurry to finish her rounds so she could leave on vacation.

The old man could hardly swallow, and his hand shook most of the water from the plastic glass.

"My toes hurt awful!" he told her.

She recalled pulling up the bandages and looking at the big toes that had turned almost completely black from lack of circulation.

"These look like toe jam," she'd remarked to the old man in a feeble attempt to be funny and get his mind on something else.

It had not been a laughing matter to the old man.

"Please give me something for the pain!" he begged her. "They hurt so bad, I can't stand it!"

She had scanned his chart to see if the doctor had left any orders for pain medication. He hadn't. She would have to call him and that would take precious minutes from her schedule. The doctor did not always return his calls promptly. She considered what to do.

She had glanced at her watch and seen she was running late. She'd been annoyed that she had one more thing to deal with when her shift was about to end. She'd quickly checked the old man's vital signs and recorded them on his chart. They hadn't changed much since the last check.

"OOHHH!" the old man had moaned, drawing his legs up tightly against his body and rocking from side to side. "Please give me something!"

"I'll call the doctor and ask if he will prescribe something to ease you," she'd promised as she'd hurried from the room to the nurses' station.

She had dialed the doctor's number, but she'd been unable to get through. She'd had not time to keep trying. His line was often busy indefinitely. She often thought he took the phone off the hook so he wouldn't be bothered. She needed to leave on time so she could get home and get ready for vacation. She had to leave early in the morning, and she'd had no time to pack. She knew she would only get a few hours sleep that night at best.

She'd heard the old man cry out again down the hall.

"Nurse!" he'd called. "Please help me!"

"I'm not answering him," she had said to herself. "These old people are never satisfied. They are always wanting something! Most of them can't even pay for what they get. They're on Medicare or Medicaid, but they expect to be treated like royalty."

She'd hastily scribbled on the chart: Called doctor for pain medication at 10:50 PM. She'd neglected to note that the doctor had not returned the call.

She had rushed to collect her purse and coat. Another nurse was coming on this shift. She would check the old man and call the doctor. Then the old man would get something for the pain. She'd put it out of her mind as she reached for her time card and punched out.

How could she have known what would happen? How could she have known that the nurse on the next shift would read the chart and think the old man had received pain medication? How could she have predicted that the old man would slip into a coma and that the nurse would think he was finally sleeping and decide not to disturb him? Tasha felt it was not her fault that the old man had gone all through the night and morning without any water or medication for the pain in his rotting toes! She had done her job! She couldn't be responsible for what happened when she was not there!

Yet the nursing home director had called her in and questioned her when she returned to work from vacation this morning. She told Tasha that the morning after she left, the old man's daughter came to visit him and found him dead. She had been very upset and threatened legal action against the home. The director didn't actually accuse Tasha of any wrong doing, but she said they were investigating.

Tasha expressed her concern, but she found the whole thing very unpleasant. She was secretly glad that she had been away when all of this took place.

Now that she was back, she was assigned to the same floor. Her first job was to make up the old man's empty bed. She thought it was odd that with the shortage of beds and the long waiting lists of patients for the nursing home, the old man's bed was still unoccupied. She mentioned it at the nurses' station, but the staff seemed reluctant to discuss it with her. As she started down the hall, she overheard two nurses near the empty room whispering about moans coming from there. They saw her listening and hurried away.

Tasha stood before the closed door, straining to hear any noise before going inside to make up the bed. She began to feel foolish. The room was quiet, so she pushed the door open and crossed to the bed. She noticed that, even though the window was closed, the room felt icy. She tried to concentrate on her tasks at hand. She put clean sheets on the mattress and pillowcases on the pillows. Then she folded a blanket and placed it across the foot of the bed.

As Tasha smoothed the bed, she felt something move under the blanket. Startled, she drew back her hand and looked down. There was nothing there!

"This room is giving me the creeps," she said to herself. "I've got to get out of here."

She turned from the bed and started toward the door. That's when she heard it!

"OOHHH!"

The moan came from the bed. She whirled around and, at first, she saw nothing.

"OOHHH!" she heard again.

Her heart was pounding. She backed to the door and gripped the doorknob. She tried to twist it, but it wouldn't turn. Horrified, Tasha watched a body slowly materialize on the bed.

"He can't be here," her reason told her. "The old man is dead!"

She turned toward the door and shook it as hard as she could, but it wouldn't budge. The moans sounded again, right behind her. Again she faced the bed, but the sight paralyzed her with fear. This couldn't be happening, but it was! The body was floating across the room straight toward her, feet first!

Her mouth flew open to scream for help, but she never got the chance. Two black toes separated from those floating feet and shot like bullets into Tasha's open mouth. One behind the other, those black toes jammed in her throat.

Tasha grabbed her throat as she slid to the floor, struggling to breathe. She knew that by the time they found her, it would be too late!

The Touch

Mary was a young country girl who didn't get to go many places, so she was very excited when her mother said she could go stay a few days with her sister, brother-in-law, and brand new nephew! Her father took her in the wagon, and then headed back home before dark.

Her sister was excited about the visit, too, and eager to show off the new house as well as the new baby. Mary carried her nephew as her sister pointed out the wallpaper, the curtains, and the furniture, much of which Mary's brother-in-law had made.

"Of course, we didn't build the house," Mary's sister told her, "but we did cut off half of the long back porch and make it into a little bedroom. We thought you might like to sleep out there. It's the coolest room in the house. There's nothing to block the breeze coming down the hollow."

"It's great!" said Mary. And it was until she saw the scene from the side window.

"You didn't tell me that you live next to a church," Mary said.

"Yes, this used to be the parsonage," her sister explained.

By then, Mary was staring out the window at the little graveyard beside the church. From her unobstructed view, Mary could see that there was one new grave. The top was covered completely with fresh cut flowers.

"Who was just buried?" Mary asked.

"Vera Gibson," her sister replied.

"What killed her?" asked Mary.

"Childbirth," her sister answered. "Her husband took the baby to his family in Ohio right after the funeral. It's so sad!"

Mary followed her sister back into the living room. Playing with her nephew seemed especially precious after hearing about the mother who died and would never have the chance to play with her child.

That night some relatives stopped by to visit after supper. By the time they left, the baby was fussy and tired from being passed back and forth. Mary could see that her sister and brother-in-law were tired, too, from the constant care of the newborn.

"I've got an idea," said Mary. "Why don't you let the baby sleep in the back room with me tonight? It's cooler there and he'll sleep better. I won't mind getting up if he cries and you can get a good night's rest."

The offer was too good to pass up. Mary took the baby with her and they all went to bed. The baby fell asleep immediately when he felt the cool breeze.

Mary went to the window to pull the curtains before she dressed for bed. She couldn't resist glancing at the graveyard. In the moonlight, the headstones looked like ghostly figures bowed in prayer beside the graves. In spite of the heat and humidity of the summer night, Mary could not keep from shivering.

When she was dressed in her nightgown, Mary opened the curtains again. This time, she dashed to bed without looking out. She fell asleep right away.

Mary didn't know what woke her. She was just suddenly awake. The room was unnaturally cold. She looked at the window, wondering if she should close it. She gasped. There on the outside looking at her was a snow white face, with dull, staring eyes. Mary couldn't scream, but the strangling sound she made with her sharp intake of breath caused the baby to stir. At the same instant, the face was gone, and so was the chill that had filled the room.

Mary patted the baby and he continued to sleep. She convinced herself that she had just imagined the face at the window. Finally she managed to sleep again, but she didn't know for how long.

She woke a second time to the baby's whimpering. When she touched him to comfort him, the coldest thing she had ever felt gripped her arm and began to pull it away from the baby! He began crying at full volume at the same time Mary started screaming! Her sister and brother-in-law raced into the room to see what was happening. Whatever had touched her, let go.

"Something touched us!" she managed to explain. "It was so cold! It was awful!"

"There's nothing here now," said her sister, trying to sooth her.

"I'll take a look outside," said her brother-in-law.

He walked outside and then stopped outside the window. He stooped and picked up something before coming back inside.

"Nobody's out there," he said, "but look at this!"

He held up one of the fresh funeral flowers from the dead mother's grave!

Homeward Bound

It was the kind of night you read about in mysteries, the kind of night when only the extremely brave or the extremely desperate—or maybe even the dead—would be out wandering about. Ruth was one of the desperate.

"Please wait until morning," her roommate begged. "It's too far to go alone at night, especially with the snow coming down already."

Ruth looked again at the message her roommate had given her. It was incomplete, but there was enough information for Ruth to know she was needed at home.

Home was her grandmother's farm in the foothills of the Appalachian Mountains, about two hours drive from the college Ruth attended. Her grandmother and her Uncle Josh had taken her in after her parents were killed in an automobile accident when she was ten. They would never have called her if something terrible hadn't happened.

The call had come from Mr. Harmon, who ran the only general store in the neighborhood and had the only phone. The storm was already affecting the phone lines when he placed the call. All her roommate had actually heard clearly was, "Grandmother...emergency...Uncle Josh..." Of course, she tried to call Mr. Harmon back, but the lines were down by then.

"I've got to go now," she told her roommate. "I might not be able to get through tomorrow if the storm keeps up. Grandma must be dead or dying!"

"You could die yourself if you get stuck in a snowstorm alone!" argued her roommate. "Nobody knows you're coming, so they wouldn't even come looking for you!"

"I've got to go anyway," Ruth insisted. "I'll make it!"

Ruth packed hurriedly, filled up the car with gas, and headed out. She soon left the campus behind and concentrated on the open road.

Huge flakes were hitting the windshield as fast as the wipers could knock them off. She flipped on the radio as they were giving a travel advisory. She felt uneasy about that. She knew how slippery the hilly roads could get, and she knew she had to drive along long stretches without guardrails.

She slowed down, barely able to see the road now through the swirling white flakes. An hour and a half crept by. The landscape seemed strange in the storm, and she was afraid she might miss the road where she had to turn. She saw what seemed to be the right place and turned. Things seemed to be vaguely familiar, so she drove on. Her legs felt stiff and her shoulders ached as her car crawled along the winding narrow road that led to the farm.

The trees that lined the road broke the wind for a mile or so, and Ruth began to feel more confident that she would arrive at the farm without any mishaps. Then as she topped a rise, there was a sudden **crack** and a limb fell across the road in front of her. Without thinking, Ruth hit her brakes and swerved. She felt the car sliding, and after what seemed an eternity, it came to rest in a ditch.

Ruth sat there trembling, trying to think what to do. She couldn't drive out. The ditch was too deep and the banks too slick And, as her roommate had pointed out earlier, nobody was going to come looking for her because nobody knew she was coming. Even though she had filled up, she didn't think she had enough gas to keep her warm all night.

She peered into the darkness for a light, but all she saw was snow. She wondered if it would drift and bury the car with her in it. She didn't want to be buried alive when she was only a mile or so from home, so she decided to get out and walk.

She was dressed warmly, but she wasn't prepared for the blast of icy wind that bit her face as she stepped out of the car. She gasped for breath as she tried to shield her face and get her bearings.

Nothing was as she remembered it, but it seemed wise enough just to follow the road. She looked back after a few minutes and saw that the snow and the night had already swallowed the car. She had to go on now.

She didn't know how long she walked. The snow had blown into such deep drifts that she couldn't tell if she was on the road now or not. She slipped several times and nearly fell. Each time, she stood still to steady herself. The last time, she had to admit to herself that she was hopelessly lost. She was also very cold, tired, and sleepy.

"I need to sit down and rest for just a minute," she said to herself.

She knew that was a very dangerous thing to do. When her Uncle Josh had taken her hunting or just walking in the woods, he always warned her that she must never do that when it was cold. It was too easy to go to sleep and never wake up!

She kept moving, but she knew she couldn't keep going much longer. She realized she'd done a stupid thing to come out alone on a night like this.

The wind had picked up and was howling now. It whipped the wool scarf Ruth was trying to hold over her face. She didn't know what to do next. She was beginning to fear that she would never come out of this predicament alive.

And that's when she saw him. Her Uncle Josh stepped out of a white wall of snow carrying his old red lantern. Of all the times she had seen him with that light, it had never been so beautiful. His mackinaw was buttoned and snow covered, and his hat was pulled down over his ears. He had tucked his pants into his heavy boots.

"Maybe my roommate got through with a message that I was on my way," thought Ruth, "or maybe he figured I'd head home and he'd come to meet me."

Ruth tried to ask about her grandmother, but the wind carried her voice away. He shook his head and pointed to his ears. Then he motioned for her to follow him. Seeing him renewed her strength and she concentrated on keeping up with him.

They seemed to walk forever. Ruth didn't recognize anything in the snow. When she'd get too far behind, he'd stop and wait until she caught up. In a way, it was like old times when she used to follow him around the farm. Her feet felt numb, but she kept stubbing along in sight of him.

Suddenly she recognized the pine thicket by her grandmother's pasture. Then the cherry tree took form. Just down the lane, a light shown from the farmhouse window. She ran then, leaving her uncle standing in the snow. She yelled her grandmother's name and banged on the door. She couldn't wait any longer to find out what had happened to her.

The door flew open and her grandmother stood in the circle of light from the lamp. As Ruth rushed into her arms, she could see streaks of tears on her cheeks.

"What's wrong, Grandma?" Ruth asked her. "I'm here and I'm safe now that Uncle Josh led me home."

She held Ruth tighter and began to sob. Then she held her at arm's length and looked into her eyes.

"What are you talking about, Child?" she asked. "Your Uncle Josh was killed in a logging accident today!"

"That's impossible!" said Ruth. "I couldn't have made it here without him. He's coming right behind me!"

Ruth whirled and looked around. The only tracks coming out of the dark, snow-filled lane were her own.

The Haunting of Damron's Creek

When Mike and Fanny Dean were first married, they rented a house beside Damron's Creek, not too far from where they both grew up. Fanny was only about eighteen at the time, but she was used to staying alone while the men in the family worked in the fields, sometimes until well after dark. She was never afraid.

Her landlady was Mrs. Withers, a middle-aged widow who lived across an open field in plain sight of the rental property by the creek.

"I know Mike will be late getting home sometimes when he's helping other farmers," Mrs. Withers told Fanny, "so I'll always keep a light in my window when you're here by yourself. Remember you can come to my house anytime you are scared."

Fanny thought it was odd that Mrs. Withers would think she'd be afraid.

"Thank you," said Fanny, "but there's nothing scary here."

Mrs. Withers just gave her a faint smile and went home.

Autumn came, and the days grew shorter. Mike and the other farmers helped each other harvest their crops. On days when Mike worked on other farms, it was dark before he'd get home. Mrs. Withers kept her word about keeping a light in her window. Fanny could look across the field and see it burning. Even though she wasn't afraid, it gave her a warm, friendly feeling to see it. She didn't feel the need to go over there—at least not at first.

As the days got shorter, Fanny began to notice that shadows inside the house began to look strange and sinister. She began to feel uneasy and began to take some comfort in the light across the field. She tried to ignore it, but she had to admit to herself that there was something not quite right about the house.

One day right before dusk, the house was filling fast with shadows. Mike was working on another farm and Fanny cooked supper early so the wood stove would cool down before bedtime. There were no screen doors, so Fanny covered the food with a white tablecloth to keep the flies off. It looked ghostly in the shadows. She walked to the front door to see if she could see Mike coming, but there was no sign of him.

Suddenly behind her, the house filled with whispers! She whirled around, but there was nothing to explain the sounds. The voices were close, but she couldn't understand what they were saying. The whispers, the shadows, and the white tablecloth were too much. Fanny ran outside and sat on the old rail fence by Damron's Creek until Mike came home.

"Must have been the wind," Mike said when she told him about the voices.

Fanny knew better. After that, she heard the whispering every night when she was alone. Mike would usually find her sitting on the fence. If it were too stormy or cold to be outside, Fanny would move her chair next to the door and sit and wait. Mike found it amusing and he was just about to convince her that she was imagining things when the unforgettable happened.

It was just about dark, but the sun was still bright enough to light up the yard. Fanny finished cooking supper and decided she'd sweep the porch while she waited for Mike. She caught a glimpse of someone walking through the yard and thought Mike had come home early. She looked around to tell him supper was ready, and what she saw nearly made her keel over!

The man walking through the yard wasn't Mike. This man was wearing a dark suit, a white shirt, and a fancy tie. That was odd because people on Damron's Creek only dressed up in suits to go to church on Sunday or to attend a funeral. She stared because of something else, though. Right up above that tie, there was absolutely nothing. The man had no head!

Fanny didn't remember where the man went or how she got to Mrs. Withers' house. She practically fell through her front door. After having a cup of tea, Fanny finally managed to tell what had happened.

Mrs. Withers listened without too much surprise.

"I'm not crazy!" Fanny told her. "I saw a headless man!"

"I believe you," Mrs. Withers said quietly. "I've heard it from others."

"Please tell me what you know!" Fanny pleaded. "I can't be any more frightened than I am now!"

"Well, it is tragic, but I'll tell you what I know," said Mrs. Withers.

Fanny pulled her chair close so she would not miss a word.

"Before I married and moved to this house, the area around Damron's Creek was a favored site for moonshining. Bill Damron was known for it far and wide. People came by land and a few by boat on the creek to get the best tasting moonshine a still could turn out. From time to time though, there were bloody skirmishes fought between the moonshiners and the revenuers. Then there was a new sheriff elected. He vowed to shut down all the stills and put an end to illegal moonshining once and for all. When he raided Bill Damron's place, Bill put up the fight of his life. The sheriff had brought dynamite to blow up the still, and Bill tried to stop it. The sheriff set off the charge just as Bill ran up to remove it. The blast blew up the still, and it blew Bill Damron's head completely off!

People have talked in whispers for years that Bill Damron will never stay in his grave until he finds his head."

"Oh, Lord," said Fanny. "Do you think that's who I saw?"

"I don't know," said Mrs. Withers. "He was buried in a dark suit, white shirt, and fancy tie."

"Oh, were you at the funeral?" asked Fanny. "Did you know him?"

"Yes," said Mrs. Withers. "I hope he finds peace. You see, he was my father."

Mike and Fanny found another place soon after this and moved away. To this day, there are stories of a headless man walking along Damron's Creek!

The Boundary Oak

In south central Kentucky, a majestic oak tree stands alone, marking the boundary line between two farms. Some folks say it is also a boundary between this world and the next. Most of them stay clear of it, especially at sunset.

Steve Simpson and Sam Stephens once owned the two farms separated by this tree. The boundary oak got its name when the two men had a disagreement over the boundary line. The line was actually a little stream that often changed its course when heavy rains came. Sometimes Sam had the rich bottomland along the banks of the creek, and other times Steve had it.

The dispute went unsettled until Sam decided to take it to court. The judge was Sam's good friend, so it wasn't too surprising when he ruled in Sam's favor. It was the decision of the court that the boundary line would be marked by the huge oak tree instead of the little stream. This meant that Sam would have the rich bottomland for his crops regardless of which way the stream ran.

Steve felt the ruling was unjust. The land had been in his family for generations, and he knew where the boundary should be. It was unfair, but he knew there wasn't anything he could do about it.

Sam waited for Steve outside the courtroom that day. He offered his hand, but Steve made no move to shake it.

"Looks like I won," said Sam.

"Yeah, it looks that way," Steve answered. "The land is yours now. Just make sure you stay on it. I'll never set foot on your property again, and I don't want you on mine. If I ever catch you or any of your family on my land for any reason whatsoever, I'll kill you or whoever has crossed the boundary line. I'm giving you fair warning."

Sam made no reply. He hadn't thought Steve would be so bitter. He knew he meant what he said, though. Steve always said what he meant and he always kept his word. Sam hoped Steve would change his mind when he had time to cool down, but he could take no chances. He told his family they must never go on Steve Simpson's land again.

The years went by and the two men worked their fields in view of each other. Sometimes they rested in the shade of the boundary oak, but they never crossed the property line and they never spoke.

Sam often told people it was a hollow victory he'd won in court that day. Getting that small strip of land was not worth losing a friend. Steve never let on if he heard of Sam's remorse. Things went on the same year after year.

Then came the spring that Steve's wife, Lou Ann, came down with a fever. Their children were grown and gone from home. There was nobody to take care of her except Steve. He had crops to plant, so he couldn't stay with her very much during the day.

When Sam's wife Liz heard how sick Lou Ann was, she decided to put an end to the feud that had separated the families for so long.

"Steve won't be able to take care of Lou Ann by himself," Liz told her daughter Barbara Jane. "I'm going over to see what I can do for her."

"No, Momma," she pleaded. "Please don't go over there. You know what Papa said. At least wait until he gets back from town. You know that man said he'd kill any of us who sets foot on his land."

"I'm not afraid of Steve Simpson," Liz declared. "Lou Ann used to be a friend of mine before all this nonsense got out of hand. I can't sit over here and let that poor woman die if there is anything I can do to save her."

"Then I'm going with you," declared Barbara Jane.

Liz didn't tell her she couldn't go. She really didn't think they would be in any danger. They walked across the fields toward the old oak tree without talking. Their hearts beat faster as they crossed the boundary line and started along the fence row that led to the Simpsons' farm house.

"I'm scared, Momma," said Barbara Jane.

"Then go back home," Liz told her.

"Not without you!" said Barbara Jane.

The two walked on together. Barbara Jane half expected Steve Simpson to jump from the thick bushes, but nothing stirred.

As they neared the farmhouse, they could see Steve Simpson sitting by his woodpile, sharpening his ax. For a moment, they hesitated.

Barbara Jane tugged at her mother's arm and whispered, "Let's go home before he kills us! You know he always keeps his word."

"Pay no mind to him, Barbara Jane," Liz instructed. "It's Lou Ann we've come to see. This is her land as much as it is his."

The two hardly breathed as they passed the woodpile. Steve gave no sign that he saw them. They reached the front door, relief flooding through them as they stepped inside.

They found Lou Ann moaning and tossing on her bed. She was burning with fever and didn't recognize them. Liz brewed some hot herb tea to bring down the fever. Then they looked around the room and decided what they needed to do.

They changed the bed, fluffed the pillows, bathed Lou Ann, and dressed her in a clean gown. Then they set about cleaning the house and cooking enough food to last a couple of days.

Now and then as they worked, Barbara Jane glanced out the window and saw that Steve was still by the woodpile. She was relieved when she looked again and saw that he was gone.

"Maybe you're right, Momma," she said. "Maybe he's not going to do anything. Maybe he was too ashamed of the way he's been acting to come and speak to us."

Liz smiled and nodded. For the first time since they left home, Barbara Jane relaxed.

They had some time left before they had to leave, so Liz and Barbara Jane swept the floors, carried water from the spring, washed the dirty clothes on an old wash board and hung them up to dry overnight. They set a place for Steve at the table and put the food out in covered dishes. Then they roused Lou Ann up enough to eat a little chicken soup before they started home. She was sleeping when they left.

They followed the fence row back the way they came. They admitted to each other that they felt good about what they'd done for Lou Ann.

As they walked, they could see their own house in the distance. They looked forward to getting home to a hot meal and an evening of rest.

As they reached the boundary oak, they saw a sudden movement. They stopped as Steve Simpson stepped out from behind the huge trunk and walked toward them without a word. They had no time to run. The last thing they saw was the flash of the ax in the late evening sun. Only Barbara Jane lived long enough to tell what happened.

Steve carried his bloody ax to the woodpile and left it there where he had sharpened it He entered the house and looked at Lou Ann, who was calmer now, but still feverish. He knew it was only a matter of time before the sheriff or a lynch mob would come for him. He sat at the table and ate some of the food that his two victims had just prepared.

"I told 'em not to come on my land. I told 'em what I'd do," he muttered. "A man has to keep his word. That's the only thing he's got. Christ! I told them!"

Lou Ann heard him talking, but she was too weak to understand then. She heard him get up and approach the bed. She felt his lips brush her cheek, but she didn't see him go outside to wait by the woodpile for those he knew would come. She didn't hear the men on horseback who took Steve away to hang him on the old boundary oak. She was fast asleep!

Soon after that tragic day, Sam Stephens was riding the boundary of his property at sunset, checking fences. His horse stopped suddenly and reared straight up into the air. While trying to quiet him, Sam looked around to see what the problem was that was spooking the horse. He expected to see a snake, but he noticed that the horse was looking at the boundary oak. He saw that somebody was sitting by the tree, holding an ax. He looked closer and, to his horror, he saw that it was Steve Simpson! Sam managed to turn the frightened horse and spur it the other way. He refused to go near the tree again.

LAMPLIGHT TALES

Many folks that passed the old boundary oak saw Steve Simpson sitting there with the rays of the late afternoon sun reflecting from the ax by his side. Some say that maybe he can't cross the boundary between life and death because of his evil deed. Others say he may come back to get even with those who took his life. Most people agree on one thing, though. As the sun starts to set and the shadows creep in, nobody wants to be near the old boundary oak.

Crying in the Rain

The day seemed too normal for such a strange thing to happen. Lillian Dean had gone to visit her Uncle Golce and Aunt Cood to help them get settled on their new farm.

Her two older cousins were boys and not much help to Aunt Cood in the house.

Lillian was hanging curtains when she noticed a gentle rain had set in. It fell steadily as darkness settled around the old farmhouse. The family ate supper and, after the dishes were done, they all gathered in the parlor to talk until bedtime.

The night was calm and the steady patter of rain on the roof was soothing. There was no thunder or lightning to conjure up spooky images, and they were not telling scary tales. They were catching up on family news when, during a lull in the conversation, they heard a low whimpering sound outside the front door.

"Is that a dog, boys?" Golce asked his sons.

The boys shook their heads.

"No," they said. "We haven't seen one around."

The talk started up again, but the whimpering got louder. This time, the door rattled slightly, too.

"Must be the wind picking up," said Cood.

"No," said Golce, shaking his head. "The wind's not blowing."

They looked at each other, but nobody moved. The sound had changed, and it was clear to all of them now that a baby was outside, crying in the rain! It was hard to believe, since there was no baby in the family, or even in the neighborhood, as far as they knew.

As they sat staring at the door, the wooden latch that held the door shut began to move slowly.

"We must be getting company," said Golce, "but I didn't hear a knock."

Before he could get up from his chair, the latch lifted all the way and the door swung open. By the lamplight, they saw a lily-white hand reach inside, touch the door casing, and then vanish!

They looked at each other, shocked, but they still thought a woman and baby were outside. They waited for the visitor to bring the crying baby inside where it was dry. Seconds ticked by, but nobody knocked or came in. Everybody followed Golce to the porch to see what was going on, but the porch was empty. There were no tracks in the yard. They could still hear the baby crying, but now it seemed to be coming from the big rain barrel beside the house. Golce lit a lantern and looked inside, but the barrel held nothing but water. They knew no baby could be alive in there, yet the sound was so convincing that Golce and the boys emptied the barrel. When the barrel was empty, the sound seemed to come from the ground beneath it. They all stared wild-eyed at each other.

"Turn the barrel over, boys," said Golce.

The boys turned it, but the undisturbed earth showed them that nothing had been buried there recently.

"This is not of the living," said Cood. "Put the barrel back and come inside."

The boys turned the barrel upright and they all went back into the house. They went to bed and tried to sleep, but the rain drummed a steady beat and the crying continued. Then as the old grandfather clock struck midnight, both stopped. It was only then that their sleepy eyelids stayed closed.

When morning came, Golce and Cood had a fire going and breakfast cooked when Lillian and the boys woke up. They ate as fast as they could and then they ran out to see if they could find any clues to solve the mystery of last night's visitors. They only found tracks made by the family.

After Lillian went home, Golce's family saw the white hand and heard the crying several times, but only on rainy nights!

When Golce got to know his neighbor fairly well, he told him about the hand and the crying.

"Did you ever hear about this from the people who lived here before we bought the place?" Golce asked the man.

"I've heard about it," the neighbor nodded. "It's a story that dates all the way back to the Civil War. Names and details are long lost in time."

"Tell me the story anyway," urged Golce.

"Well," said the man, "the man who owned the farm left his wife and baby and went off to fight for the South. Yankee soldiers came through one rainy night and sought shelter in the farmhouse. A neighbor slipped over to see what was going on, but there was nothing she could do without putting herself in danger. The soldiers were drinking and, as the night wore on, they got loud and wild. The baby got scared and began to cry. It wouldn't hush, so some of the drunken soldiers took it out and drowned it in the rain barrel. The mother fought them, but they hit her on the head and killed her, too. That's when the neighbor sneaked away home, so she never knew what they did with the bodies.

They were never found, so the Yankee soldiers were never punished. They said the young husband was killed in battle and never came home."

"Do you think the soldiers buried the mother and baby under the rain barrel?" asked Golce.

"They wouldn't have left on foot carrying two dead bodies, now would they?" asked the neighbor. "Of course, the rain barrel wasn't always where it is now, so there is little chance of finding their bones."

Sometime on a night when the wind cries and the rain streams down widow panes like tears, a lily white hand may open a door and provide some long lost answers.

He'll Come Knocking

It was the week before Christmas when Amy first saw the house where her in-laws lived. It stood towering over the landscape in stark beauty against the threatening winter sky.

"Elmer!" she said. "You didn't tell me your family is rich!"

Elmer and Amy had married in June and moved to Cincinnati where Elmer had a job. There had been no time to drive out in the country where his parents lived. Amy was glad they had invited Elmer and her to visit for the Christmas holidays. She wanted to get to know them better and to spend Christmas in the country like she always had as a child.

"My parents aren't rich," he declared.

"Then how can they afford a house like this one?" she asked.

"You'll see soon enough," he said.

Amy could not get him to say anything else about the house.

The view was spectacular in every direction, with hills and trees and rolling fields. It was so pretty, Amy hesitated to enter the house, even when Elmer's mom and dad ran out to greet them.

Inside, the house was warm and cozy, but the furnishings were not nearly as fancy as one would expect to see in such a grand house.

Elmer's mom led them to a front bedroom on the first floor. Elmer looked surprised.

"Can't we sleep upstairs?" he asked.

"No, it's too cold," she said. "We've closed the upstairs off for the winter. With snow coming, the temperature will drop close to zero."

"I'd rather not stay in this room," Elmer told her.

"Elmer!" said Amy. "This is a perfect room! We'll sleep where it's convenient for your mom!"

"You'll be fine here," she said. "You'll be in the parlor with us most of the time anyway."

She left them to unpack while she put supper on the table. As soon as she was gone, Amy turned to Elmer.

"Why on earth did you tell your mom that you would rather not stay in this room?" she asked.

"You'll see soon enough," he said again. And again, he refused to discuss it anymore.

Amy couldn't understand his attitude. The room was large and cheerful. She had noticed as they came in that there were glass doors leading to this room, but now that she was inside she saw that two thick oak doors covered this entrance, too. Amy started to open them to see the view, but Elmer spoke sharply as she reached to unlock them.

"Don't open those doors," he ordered. "Especially not tonight!"

"Why?" she asked, bewildered.

"It's going to snow," he said in a calmer voice.

"All the better!" said Amy. "We can watch it come down. It will be beautiful!"

Before he could answer, his mom called them to supper. They left the room and the thick doors stayed locked.

The food was delicious, and they sat by the fire talking after Elmer's mom and Amy did the dishes. The curtains were open at the big front window, so they saw the first snow flakes begin about eight o'clock. Within the next hour, the wind picked up and began whirling the snow into spooky shapes in the yard. Even though the fire burned brightly, Amy felt a chill creep into her bones.

"I hope you will excuse me," she said, "but I'm more exhausted from the trip than I thought. I think I'll go on to bed."

"Wait," exclaimed Elmer. "I thought we might sing some carols or something."

Amy didn't know that Elmer liked carols, but she did know that she wasn't up to singing tonight.

"We'll do that tomorrow night when I'm rested," she told him. "I really do need to get some rest."

"Then I'll turn in, too," he said.

"No," she said, "Stay up and visit with your parents as long as you want to."

His father stood up.

"I think we should all try to get some sleep," he said. "We can visit in the morning."

Amy was too tired to suggest opening the doors. She fell asleep to the sound of the wind wailing around the house and rattling the windows. She slept deeply for about an hour, when a different sound woke her. Someone was pounding on the oak doors to the room. Somehow they had managed to get the glass doors open!

"Elmer, wake up!" said Amy. "Someone's out there in the snow!"

"Shhh!" he whispered. "I'm awake. Be still!"

"But Elmer!" protested Amy. "There's a blizzard out there. We've got to see who it is and let them in!"

She threw back the covers and started to get out of bed. Elmer grabbed her shoulders and held her.

"I know who's out there," Elmer said, still whispering. "Now be quiet until he's gone!"

"But he'll freeze to death!" Amy whispered back.

"He already has!" Elmer answered sadly.

"What are you talking about?" asked Amy. "Are you crazy?"

Just as the meaning of Elmer's words sank in, the knocking grew louder. The powerful force of each blow shook the heavy doors until Amy was sure they would give way. Then the doorknobs began to rattle, but the locks held firm.

Amy clung to Elmer for the next few minutes until the knocking stopped. Outside, the wind died down and the snow fell undisturbed.

Elmer lit a candle and propped up their pillows. It was obvious he was ready to talk. Amy glanced at the clock and saw that it was about ten minutes past ten.

"Now do you see why I didn't want to sleep in here?" he asked her.

"Yes," she said, her teeth chattering from the experience she had just gone through. "I'd rather sleep upstairs for the rest of our visit, even if there isn't any heat."

"We won't need to unless there's another snow storm.," said Elmer. "He only comes on snowy, blustery nights."

"Why?" asked Amy. "Who is he?"

"The ghost of Brutus Jackson," said Elmer. "And as sure as there is a snow storm, he'll come knocking."

"A ghost knocks at the door?" Amy said.

"I told you there was a reason my parents could afford this house," said Elmer. "You've just seen why."

"But who is Brutus Jackson and what has he got to do with this house?" Amy wanted to know.

"He's the man who built this house for his new bride a long time ago," Elmer explained. "He brought her all the way from Mississippi. Her family thought he was a good catch. He was rich and strong, and they thought the poor girl would have a good living. What they didn't know was that he loved to drink, and he always turned vicious when he did. When he'd go on one of his binges, he'd beat his wife, even when she was carrying their child."

"Why did she put up with that?" asked Amy.

"She had no family here," said Elmer, "and Brutus saw to it that she had no money to travel. She finally stood up to him when he came home drunk and started to beat their newborn baby. The temperature had just reached freezing when he came home that night. The wind howled and whipped the snow like it did tonight. When she told him she wanted to go back to her family in Mississippi, he opened the glass doors right here in this room and ordered her to take the baby and go. She pretended that she was going to bundle up the baby, but instead she pushed him out the doors and locked them behind him. He knocked and pounded, but she was afraid to let him in. Finally the cold and the whiskey made him sleepy. He sat down beside the doors and froze to death by morning."

"How tragic!" said Amy. "What happened to her?

"There was a hearing in court, but everybody agreed that she had only killed him in self-defense. She took her baby and moved back to Mississippi."

"Did your parents buy the house from her?" Amy asked.

"No," said Elmer. "A couple named Holmes bought it. During the first snow storm that year, they woke to the pounding. Mr. Holmes opened the glass doors and was pulled into the snow by some invisible force. His wife could see there was some awful struggle, but she couldn't stop it until she grabbed the Bible and began to pray. Whatever it was let Mr. Holmes go. His wife helped him inside, but he took pneumonia from the exposure and never recovered. My parents bought the house from Mrs. Holmes. She took the first offer because she just wanted to get away."

"Who put up the oak doors?" asked Amy.

"My father did that," said Elmer. "He added extra locks. So far, they've always held off the ghost of Brutus Jackson when he comes knocking."

There were no more snow storms during that Christmas holiday, so they spent it peacefully as it should be spent. But after that, Elmer and Amy always planned their visits during spring or summer.

Night Walkers

J. R. Russell loved to walk in the dark. When his mom and dad would go to sleep at night, J. R. would cautiously open the window, pause to be sure the sound did not wake them, and then step out on the garage roof beside his room. From there, it was only a few steps to the big maple tree, from which he could easily climb to the ground.

Most of the time, he could take his walk and climb back into his room without anyone knowing he'd been gone. If he got caught, it was usually on a stormy night when the wind or thunder woke his mother.

"J. R.," she'd scold, "you must not walk by yourself at night. You don't know what you might run into out there."

"I'm sorry, Mom," he'd tell her. "I won't do it anymore."

J. R. meant to keep his word. He didn't want to worry her and he didn't mean to lie, but he couldn't resist the urge to walk when dark came. It tugged at his thought relentlessly. He would toss and turn and watch the shadows dancing at his window. They reached out beckoning to him like giant hands. He couldn't hold out for more than a few nights, and then he'd be out walking again.

J. R. was proud that he was not afraid of the dark like some kids he knew. Donald Richards, who lived on the corner, never played outside after sunset. And Beverly Oldham, who lived across the street, never walked in the dark alone. She had asked him to walk her home one night when she had stayed at his house until after dark.

"See?" he said with a superior air when they had safely reached her door. "There's nothing in the dark to be afraid of!"

"Yes, there is," she insisted. "There are night walkers!"

"Night walkers?" repeated J. R.

Beverly nodded solemnly.

"What are night walkers?" J. R. asked, amused by Beverly's serious attitude.

Beverly saw the amusement in his eyes and didn't appreciate it.
"Any fool knows that night walkers are the dead!" she informed him. "They walk at night to catch people alone so they can turn them into night walkers. When they find others to replace themselves, they can rest!"

J. R. threw back his head and laughed. Beverly, red-faced and furious, stormed inside.

"How come I've never met any at night when I'm out walking?" he called after her. Her only answer was a slam of the door.

J. R. was still laughing as he crossed the street, but about half way home he got a creepy feeling. For the first time in his life, he felt he was not alone in the dark! And, for the first time, he hurried inside.

"You've let a girl spook you," he told himself. "There's nothing to be afraid of."

It was enough, however, to keep J. R. inside for a few nights, though he would never admit it.

Beverly's words were totally forgotten when his parents announced that they were going to their favorite lake resort for the weekend. Surely there would be an opportunity to go walking there.

J. R. and his parents arrived at the lake resort about 2 P.M. and checked into the lodge. J. R. was delight to learn that his parents had reserved a suite with a separate room for him. That would make it easier to sneak out for a walk if he got the urge later.

His parents thought about his walking, too. They had hoped to curb any such impulse by tiring him out that afternoon. They scheduled a hike along the lake with several other guests and a trail guide. That wasn't as good as walking alone, but J. R. suspected what they had in mind and agreed to go.

Birds twittered nervously from the trees along the trail and little creatures scurried unseen to the safety of the weeds and grass, disturbed by the presence of the hikers.

J. R. wondered what the trail would be like in the dark. He tried to imagine the sounds he'd hear if he came alone at night. He was fairly confident that he would have a chance to find out. His mom and dad would probably be so exhausted from the hike that they would go to bed right after dinner. With that in mind, he began to pay more attention to the guide and to the surroundings so he wouldn't get lost when he came back alone later.

The guide stopped the group near an old dock that was in obvious need of repair.

"As you can see by the signs," he said," this dock is off limits. We ask that you please stay away from it."

J. R.'s interest was immediately sparked.

"Why don't you fix it?" he asked.

The guide looked uncomfortable.

"Repairs are expensive and we don't really need it," he answered. "Now I'd better get you back to the lodge so you won't miss your dinner!"

J. R. wondered why it made the guard uncomfortable to talk about the dock. He made a mental note to find out.

J. R. gulped his food at dinner and finished long before his parents. He sat staring toward the old dock. From the window, he could see an old man fishing from the bank.

His parents couldn't see him from where they were sitting. They told him never to talk to strangers, but this old man looked harmless. He might have information about the dock.

"Is it okay if I walk down to the lake for a while?" J. R. asked casually.

His parents exchanged glances, hesitated, and finally nodded their permission. He was out of his seat in a flash.

J. R. approached the lake and sat down quietly on the bank, leaving a comfortable distance between himself and the old fisherman. The old man smiled and J. R. smiled back.

"Done any fishing in these parts?" the old man asked.

"No, Sir," said J. R.

"Good place," said the man.

"Did you ever fish at that old dock?" asked J. R.

"Yes, but it's unsafe now." he answered. "Most people stay away from it."

"Why?" J. R. asked.

"Oh, it's because of something that happened a long time ago," said the old man. "It would just bore a young fellow like you."

"No, it wouldn't," said J. R. "I'd like to hear about it."

"Well, son," said the man, "not everybody around here wanted the dam built to form this lake. A lot of families had lived here for years on farms handed down generation after generation. There was one man who didn't want to sell his land. He watched the farms around him being bought up one by one until only his farm was left. He was determined not to be forced out."

"What did he do?" asked J. R.

"Oh, he held out as long as he could," said the old man. "Finally he lost to progress. The government took his land for what it considered a fair price. They forced him off his land, built the dam, and covered all these acres with water."

"What's that got to do with the old dock?" asked J. R.

"Well, the fellow was pretty upset about losing his land," said the man, so one night he came down to that dock. It wasn't old then, of course. Several boats were tied up there, so he took one and rowed out to the center of the lake. A storm was coming up and several fishermen on shore called for him to stop. He never answered. He just kept rowing."

"What happened to him?" asked J. R.

"The storm hit, so nobody could look for him right away. They searched after the storm was over, but they never found him. He was gone without a trace. People around here say there are catfish in this lake big enough to swallow a man. They think maybe that's what happened," the old man continued.

"Did they ever find the boat?" J. R. asked.

"Not right away," the man told him. "They figured it was broken up by the storm. But a couple of days later, it was tied up at that old dock, the bottom all covered in mud like it had been on the very bottom of the lake."

"I don't see why they would declare the dock off limits because of that!" exclaimed J. R.

"Well hold on, son," said the old man. "I haven't finished the story. That boat would disappear and reappear at that dock for no reason. People claimed to see a mysterious boatman at the dock at night and they figured it was the old farmer's ghost. A death always followed the appearance of the boatman. People stayed away from the dock and they let it rot and ruin."

The old man stopped talking and sat staring across the lake. J. R. shivered. He suddenly felt uneasy.

"I've got to go now," he told the old man. "Thanks for the story. I'll see you later."

"I'm afraid you will, son," he said. "I'm afraid you will."

A sad look crossed his face as he looked at J. R.

J. R. turned and ran all the way to the lodge. The old man's words kept echoing in his mind. What could he have meant? It sounded like a warning! J. R. didn't look back until he was safely inside the lobby. He quickly crossed to the window and looked toward the lake. There was no sign of the old man anywhere.

J. R. turned from the window and went directly to his parents' room. They were in bed watching TV. J. R. started to tell them the old man's story, but decided he might get in trouble for talking to strangers. Instead, he told them he was going to bed and watch TV in his room.

He debated whether to walk or not. Part of him wanted to go to sleep, safe in his bed. Another part of him wanted to see the old dock in the moonlight! Finally, he knew he had to go.

It was a little before midnight when J. R. eased his door open and closed it quietly behind him. He tiptoed down the hall and across the lobby. The desk clerk was talking on the phone and paid no attention to him.

A chilly breeze started as J. R. stepped outside He could feel the damp through his thin shirt as he walked along the lake. Shadows loomed all around him, and, for the first time, he didn't like them.

He could see the dock ahead now, but it wasn't deserted! He could see something bobbing in the water. It was a boat with a dark figure sitting in it!

The figure turned and J. R. saw with relief that it was the old fisherman he'd talked to earlier. The boards on the dock looked sound in the pale moonlight, so J. R. rushed out on the dock to say hello. Too late, he heard the crack as the boards gave way! He plunged into the cold, inky water of the lake. Down, down, down he went with nothing to grab onto. Then he felt something take hold of his arm, and he felt himself rising.

When his head broke the surface, he saw that it was the old fisherman. Then he felt himself being pulled into the boat.

J. R. looked up to thank him, but his mouth froze. The rotting stench of death filled the air and he could not breathe. The old man's face drew near, and the bloated lips spoke.

"I like you, son," he said. "I was afraid you'd come when you heard my story. I have decided not to take you down to my farm."

J. R. didn't remember much about what happened next. As the boat drifted to shore, he drifted into sleep. He awoke much later in a hospital room with his parents beside his bed.

"I want to go home," he said. "I want to tell Donald Richards that he was right not to play outside after dark and I want to tell Beverly Oldham that she was right about the night walkers."

Draculanterns

Professor Parker bought the old place next to the little community church and moved there when he retired from some university in the Midwest. He didn't know much about farming, but he planted a pumpkin patch in the field beyond the barbed wire fence that ran along the road. He announced to all the people passing by on their way to church that he was going into the pumpkin business.

The topsoil in the field had eroded away, so the vines bore a few pumpkins. The professor needed a supply of rich soil close at hand, so he decided his best source was the dirt in the graveyard. People were shocked when they found out

"Good Lord!" his neighbor told him. "Everybody knows not to disturb the soil that covers the dead. They'll come back!"

"And do what?" laughed the professor.

"I wouldn't take it too lightly," a neighbor told him. "Everybody knows that graveyard dirt is cursed."

The professor ignored the warnings. Signs of digging were seen in the graveyard, and an unusual crop of pumpkins was soon seen in the pumpkin patch.

At harvest time, the professor did a profitable business. The bright orange pumpkins were large and almost perfectly round. The Professor carved faces on them himself. Each one had long fangs like Dracula, so he called them Draculanterns instead of Jack-O - Lanterns. Every kid in the country had to have one.

"I don't think the curse is working," bragged Professor Parker. "All those families bought my Draculanterns and not one bad thing has happened to them. Best of all, I've made quite a profit! I think I'll go home and make a pumpkin pie to celebrate!"

Two days went by and neighbors began to worry because nobody had seen the professor. Some of the men got together with the doctor and went over to check on him. They found him slumped in his chair. When the doctor examined him, he found that a small piece of pumpkin had lodged in his throat and choked him to death. On the table was a Draculantern he had been carving for a centerpiece. The left fang was missing.

The community was surprised that the professor had willed the farm to the church. The congregation voted to use the land for much-needed expansion of the cemetery. Most of them think that the dead who were disturbed had their revenge and are back in the graves. Nothing is planted in the graveyard now, but now and then a pumpkin vine will come up on its own and produce a few pumpkins. People leave them on the vine to rot. It's better to leave the dead among the dead.

Fishing Creek Hill

It was a cold, rainy night and fog was settling in along Fishing Creek Hill. Henry Sims was on his way home from visiting his brother who lived about thirty miles away. He was beginning to wish he hadn't started out on a night like this, especially since this was his first car. He hadn't realized night driving would be so difficult. He'd driven in rain before without any problems, but this fog was something new and different. He was needed at home, though. His mother's call had come right at nightfall. His father had hurt his foot and needed to go to the doctor, so Henry had started home.

As Henry drove, he leaned forward and strained to see the road. The first twenty miles went by in slow motion as he kept his eyes on the white line that guided him along.

Fishing Creek Hill was coming up now, and he began to remember all the weird stories he'd heard about this place while he was growing up. There were tales of a ghost that hitch hiked a ride with travelers and then just disappeared at the top of the hill. He had always laughed at such stories, but tonight they didn't seem so funny. The fog swirled into ghostly, ever-changing shapes!

As Henry approached the bridge over Fishing Creek, car lights suddenly came from nowhere on his side of the road. Henry's instincts took over. He swerved sharply to the right and found himself bouncing around as the car rolled down the embankment and stopped with the front wheels in the creek. He was shaken, but a quick check of himself determined that nothing was broken.

Henry pushed the car door open and scrambled up the bank. The rain had picked up and was coming down with a steady beat now. Henry could feel the fog seep into the pores of his skin. His coat offered little warmth now that it was getting wet. He reached the road and thought surely the driver who ran him off the road would have stopped. No car was there. He'd have to walk for help or hitch hike.

Then it occurred to him that it might be difficult to convince a driver to stop on Fishing Creek Hill. Anybody who saw him would think that he was the ghostly hitchhiker!

Henry knew he couldn't just stand there, but there were no house lights visible through the dense fog. He felt like crying as he stood by the bridge trying to decide what to do.

He was startled when a small voice behind him said, "Are you hurt, sir?"

He turned around and was surprised to see a boy about ten years old holding a fishing pole. He wondered why a boy would be out fishing alone on a night like this.

"I'm just shook up," he told the boy. "I need some help getting my car our of the creek."

"My dad will help you," said the boy. "Come on with me."

The boy was barely visible in the fog as Henry hurried behind him. In a few minutes, Henry could see the lights from a house. The boy approached the door and knocked. It opened immediately. Henry was facing a large, white-faced man.

"You in trouble, son?" he asked.

Henry quickly told him his problem.

"I think we can get you out," the man said. "Ben!" he called to someone inside the house. "Get the tractor and the chain."

Ben was a young man of about twenty. He nodded at Henry as he came through the door and disappeared around the house. In a remarkably short time, Henry's car was back on the road. Other than a few scratches and dents, the car was in good shape. Henry offered to pay, but the men wouldn't hear of it. All they would accept was his thanks.

"Where's your other son?" asked Henry. "I want to thank him, too."

A sad look crossed the older man's face.

"I'm afraid that's not possible," he said. "But he knows you're grateful."

"I don't understand," said Henry. "Did he go back to fish some more?"

"Son, do you know how Fishing Creek got its name?" he asked Henry suddenly.

"I always thought it was be cause the fishing was good," Henry replied. "Why?"

"Well, the fishing is good," the man said, "but people started calling it Fishing Creek for another reason. My son who led you up to the house loved to fish the creek from the time he could hold a pole. He'd sneak out at night and go fishing every time he got a chance. One night, rainy and foggy like tonight, he was hit by a car and knocked over that hill."

"No wonder he came to help me," said Henry. "I guess he knew how I felt,"

"Yes," he said, "he always goes to anyone hurt or stranded there and brings them to me. I nearly had a heart attack the first time it happened."

"Why?" asked Henry, puzzled.

"Because my son died in that accident that night. You aren't the only one who has seen him. Many others have seen him, too. The neighbors began calling this place Fishing Creek because my dead son keeps fishing out the injured or those in danger."

Henry drove away and never saw the family again. On rainy nights when he would find himself driving up Fishing Creek Hill, he felt a small measure of comfort. He never needed help again, but he knew the boy with the fishing pole would be there if he did.

The Woman at the Spring

When Jim Foley heard that his neighbor's daughter had died, he went over to sit up with the family. It was the custom for neighbors to bring food and help with whatever needed to be done, whether it was building a coffin or dressing the corpse. He had worked hard that day, but he didn't want the family to be alone. When some other neighbors arrived, Jim thought it best that he go on home and get some rest.

The snow that had fallen two days before still covered the ground, and the bright moonlight made the night seem like day. That was a very good thing for Jim Foley. He had not planned to come home during the night, so he had not taken a lantern with him. It would have been hard walking if the snow had not reflected the moonlight around him, but now he could see perfectly.

He walked briskly to stay warm, for the cold was mean and biting. When he came in sight of Hollis Gosser's house, his spirits lifted because he knew he was half way home.

He wondered if he should stop by and check on Mrs. Gosser and her baby, but decided not to since the house was dark. He didn't want to wake them.

He had tried to keep an eye on them while Hollis stayed in the city to work during the week. Several men did that to pay off bills when work was scarce locally. They would come home on weekends until they could quit their jobs and come home to stay.

The spring where the Gosser family got water was by the side of the road. As Jim approached, he saw a woman in a long white gown standing on the other side of the spring. When he looked closer, he saw that it was Mrs. Gosser.

He wasn't too surprised at first. If anybody got sick during the night, someone in the family would usually run to the spring for some fresh, cool water for them to drink. He thought the baby might have a fever and that she had come to get the water to try to cool it down.

"Is everything all right?" he called to her.

She shook her head and motioned for him to follow. Then she turned and rushed toward the house. Jim followed, but couldn't catch up to her. As they hurried along, he noticed that the long white gown she was wearing was a flannel nightgown. It was no wonder that she was hurrying!

She reached the house ahead of Jim and entered without waiting. He could hear the baby crying before he got to the door. Mrs. Gosser was on the bed when he went inside. Jim didn't know if she had fainted or was just trying to get warm. His first concern was to check the baby.

Jim found matches and lit the lamp. Then he picked up the baby. It didn't feel hot, but it kept crying. It was probably hungry. If Mrs. Gosser was sick, maybe she hadn't fed it.

"Mrs. Gosser," he asked, "what can I give the baby to eat?"

She didn't answer, so Jim crossed to the bed to check on her.

"Mrs. Gosser?" Jim said.

She didn't respond, so Jim reached over and touched her shoulder. She didn't respond, so he shook her gently. Then he realized she was dead. She couldn't have died just then because she was cold and stiff. She had been dead for hours, yet he had just followed her to the house from the spring minutes before!

He wrapped the baby in blankets and ran almost all the way home. Except for Hollis Gosser and his own family, he never told anyone the story. He knew nobody would believe that he had been met at the spring by the baby's dead mother!

Wildcat Cave

"Don't ever go in here by yourself," Elmer Watson told his grandson Orville. "Wildcat Cave is a deadly place!"

Elmer and Orville were standing just inside the cave listening to the spring storm outside. They had been rabbit hunting when the rain began and Elmer said the cave offered good shelter.

The entrance was on a cliff overlooking Russell Creek. It was tall enough for an average man to enter without bending down. Inside, it branched off into a large circular room. There were openings all around the room that led off in all directions. Most of the openings were two small for a grown man to get through.

"Where do they go?" Orville asked his grandfather.

"I don't know," replied Elmer. "Nobody does. They've never been explored. Some probably come to a dead end, but I think some come back to the surface again. Sometimes when a wildcat comes down close to the farms, we get together and go after it. Many times we have seen a wildcat run into the cave and then show up outside again. We think the wildcats know a way out. That's why we call it Wildcat Cave."

Elmer held up his lantern and Orville could see that these underground passages led on out of sight.

"I could fit through one of these openings," said Orville. "Do you want me to go in there and see where they go?"

"Never!" said Elmer sternly. "Let me show you something."

He led Orville to one of the openings at the back of the circular room. He picked up a rock from the cave floor and handed it to Orville.

"Reach your hand in there as far as you can and drop the rock," Elmer instructed. "Then listen and tell me if you hear it hit anything."

Orville dropped the rock and listened. Then he turned to Elmer, his eyes wide with amazement.

"I didn't hear anything," said Orville. "The rock never hit a bottom!"

"We call it a bottomless pit," said Elmer. "Now you see why you shouldn't crawl in there!"

The experience left Orville speechless, as his grandfather took out his pocket watch and checked the time.

"I guess we can be going now," he told Orville. "The rain should have stopped."

"I really like that watch, Grandpa," said Orville.

Elmer let Orville hold the watch for a minute and then he put it back in his pocket.

"I'll give it to you someday, like my grandfather gave it to me," he promised. But he never got the chance.

Not long after Orville and Elmer took shelter in the cave, a wildcat showed up at the farm. Elmer and some other farmers chased it to Wildcat Cave and followed it inside. It found another way out and got away. As the men were coming out, an unexpected thing happened.

Rocks suddenly fell from above the cave's entrance. Maybe the wildcat dislodged them or maybe the soil was loose because of the rains. In any case, a rock struck Elmer on the head, and he died in the cave's entrance.

Elmer's pocket watch was no where on him. The other farmers swore they hadn't seen it. They were honest men who would not steal. The watch must have been knocked off inside the cave.

The more Orville thought about it, the more he wanted to see if he could find that watch! One day he decided to climb up and take a look.

"Where do you think you're going?" a voice called from behind him.

Orville recognized his father's voice. He knew he wouldn't be happy about his plan.

"I was just going to look around the cave entrance to see if I could find Grandpa's watch," said Orville.

"You know how dangerous that cave is," said his father. "Don't ever go near it alone! Come on, we'll take a look by the entrance. If we don't find it, that's the end of the search."

Orville agreed because he was sure they'd find it. Most of the rocks had been cleared away. There was a clear view of the entrance, but there was no sign of the watch.

"It's not here," said his father. "Now I hope you're satisfied."

Of course, Orville wasn't. He decided to wait until his father went into town and then sneak back for another look.

One morning Orville saw his dad hitch the horses to the wagon, and he knew this was his chance.

"If I find it, he'll be proud," Orville told himself, "and if I don't find it, he'll never have to know."

When his father was out of sight, Orville called his dog Brownie and told his mother they were going for a walk. They doubled back and climbed quickly up the cliff.

Orville ventured just inside the cave entrance. Brownie whined and refused to follow. He sat on his hind legs and watched as Orville inched his way farther into the circular room.

Then, without warning, rocks began falling at the entrance. The cave went dark, and Orville heard one yelp from Brownie outside. Then there was just silence and damp darkness.

Orville fought back panic. Nobody knew he was in the cave, so they wouldn't know where to look for him. Brownie had yelped like he was hurt, and Orville had heard no more from him. He tried to think what to do. He looked around, confused. A noise in one passageway drew his attention. Something moved, and Orville thought he saw the glint of two green eyes.

"Oh, Lord, a wildcat!" he said aloud.

Whatever was there vanished, and nothing else happened for a few minutes. Orville decided his only hope for escape was to find the passage the wildcats used to get out. He would have to move carefully and see where he ended up.

As he started forward, something stopped him. It wasn't a wildcat or a rock, but it was a force that would not let him go toward the passages. Frightened, he turned and started in another direction. Again, something blocked his way. It felt like two hands in front of him, holding him back. Whichever way he turned, something intervened. Finally, he gave up and sat down near the entrance. He could feel small objects around him, left from other slides. He finally dozed off to sleep.

He didn't know how long it was until he heard voices calling him. He thought he was dreaming, but he heard Brownie bark.

"Help!" he cried. "Get me out!"

He heard digging and the scraping of rocks as they were pulled away. Then he saw light! There, looking in at him, was his father, some neighbors, and Brownie!

"Brownie came running up just as I got home," said his father. "He wouldn't let me go inside. I could see he had a cut on his leg, so I got the neighbors and we followed him. It's a good thing you didn't crawl off in one of those passages. We might never have found you."

"Something held me here. It wouldn't let me leave the entrance," said Orville. "I think it was Grandpa."

"Why?" his father asked.

"Because I found this while I waiting to be rescued," he said. "I thought it was a rock at first."

Then he held up his grandfather's pocket watch.

Pool Parties

Silas Garner never got tired of telling about the night at the pool. He hadn't even meant to go by the old Wakefield place, but it had seemed easier that night to go up and over the hill to his grandfather's house rather than follow the long road around. He could remember seeing the old Wakefield mansion in all its glory when he was just a boy. It stood at the top of the hill and towered over everything in the valley. It had seemed fitting to him that Larry and Linda Wakefield were sitting on top of the world. To him their life was a fairy tale.

Beside the Wakefield mansion was the only swimming pool in the county. Silas could hear the laughter and music floating on the night breeze. Sometimes he would climb high enough to hear the splashing of the guests diving into the pool for a swim. Silas could only swim in the creek. He was too poor to be invited to those parties.

Years passed and Linda and Larry Wakefield had a little girl named Erin. Silas often wished he had been their child. He would see them buying toys for her sometimes on Saturday, and sometimes he would see her in a little sailor dress. He thought of all the things he would buy if he had their money. Four years passed that way. Then came the night of the tragedy that made him glad to be himself.

The Wakefields were having another party. They let Erin say goodnight to the guests and put her to bed, but the music and loud voices kept her from sleeping.

The night had turned cool, so the guests had left the pool and gone inside for refreshments. Erin got out of bed and made her way to the kitchen. The cook and the maids were busy serving the guests and told her to get out of the way. Nobody noticed Erin's departure through the back door. They never knew why she wandered to the pool. Maybe she was looking for her mom and dad, or maybe she was looking for a favorite toy she thought might be outside. She must have cried out, but nobody heard the splash or her small voice. Later, when two guests went out for a midnight swim, they found her body.

Silas remembered the weeping. The whole town turned out for the funeral, but no one could bring comfort to the grieving parents. They went back to the mansion, but there was no fairy tale ending. Linda Wakefield claimed to hear her daughter calling from the pool, so Larry had it drained. There would be no more parties. Soon rumors spread that Linda had had a complete nervous breakdown. One day, Linda and Larry Wakefield packed their belongings and left the house with the empty pool.

Soon people who passed by the house said that maybe Linda Wakefield hadn't been crazy after all, for they, too, heard a little child calling. Silas didn't know if he believed it or not, but he had no intention of going by to see. Not until tonight.

A night chill had settled on the hillside. Silas was headed to his grandfather's house to spend the night. The wind picked up and Silas shivered. It was not a comfortable night to be out, so Silas decided to take the road that led by the old Wakefield place. The blowing limbs cast shadows on the road as he hurried by the dark, empty old house.

The sound came to his ears faintly at first. In fact, he wasn't sure of what he was hearing.

"Mommy!"

I couldn't be coming from the pool. Nobody ever went near the pool now, especially at night.

"Mommy!"

The voice was louder. This did not sound ghostly. This sounded like a real child. Silas stopped and listened.

"Mommy!"

It was definitely coming from the pool. Silas was a little frightened now. He wanted no encounter with a ghost, but what if some child had wandered onto the grounds of the old Wakefield place and had fallen into the empty pool? It could be hurt. He had to at least take a look.

He could see clearly by the bright moonlight. He approached the pool slowly. It was dry. He looked up and down the length of the pool, but nothing was there.

"It must have been the wind," he said aloud.

Silas turned and started back to the road. There was a splash behind him. He looked around, but there was no water.

Now I'm imaging things, he thought. It hasn't rained in days.

He walked with swift strides across the crumbling poolside patio; then something yanked on his shirt. He whirled around, but there was nobody there.

Silas looked down, and then he began to run. He told his story to his grandfather that night and he told it to anyone who would listen in the years to come. The ending was always the same. When he looked down that night, he saw something that disturbed him deeply. Beside him were wet footprints leading from the dry pool, and he always swore they were the bare, wet footprints of a small child!

Hauntspitality

When World War II broke out, Orville Cunningham joined the United States Marines to fight for his country like countless other young men of the time. He loved the tough image of the Marine Corps, and he finished his basic training with the cocky attitude that he could take on the world and that nothing could scare him. He got a short furlough to go home before being shipped overseas.

He borrowed a buddy's car and pushed it pretty hard going over the mountains.

Everything went along fine until the fan belt broke and left him stranded miles from town. He knew there wasn't any use to try to walk back. Every store and service station had been closed when he drove through a while ago.

A few flakes of snow swirled past the windshield and the sky looked like it was going to dump a ton before it was over. It was too cold to stay in the car, especially since he hadn't filled it up with gas in the last town, so he figured his best bet was to walk on up the road and hope to find a house where he could spend the night. People were known to extend hospitality to soldiers. He was in a warm uniform and had brought along an overcoat, so he set out, confident that all would be well.

He had walked about a half mile in snow that was now beginning to sting his cheeks and cause his eye to water, when he saw a light in the distance. It was a great relief, because he was beginning to have some doubts about the wisdom of his search for shelter on foot.

As he knocked on the door, he could see a young couple sitting at a table eating. The man came to the door and opened it. He looked at the uniform and stepped back so Orville could enter.

"What can we do for you, Soldier?" he asked.

"The fan belt broke on my car about half a mile down the road," Orville explained. "I need a place to stay tonight."

The woman was on her feet now, crossing to stand beside her husband.

"We have no extra room," she said.

"Yes, we do, Doreen," he said, placing his hands gently on her shoulders. "We can't turn a soldier away from our door on a night like this."

"I don't mean to impose," said Orville. "My name is Orville Cunningham. I'm on my way home for a short furlough before I ship out. I could sleep on the floor tonight."

The woman turned without a word and went to the kitchen. She returned with another plate and silverware as the man led Orville to the table.

"We are Doreen and Arnold Sims," he said. "You can sleep in Timmy's room, but let's have some supper first."

Orville wondered who Timmy was. Maybe it was a brother who had gone to war. Neither spoke of him while they ate. The man kept the conversation focused on Orville.

When they finished, Doreen cleared the table and Arnold led Orville upstairs to the room where he would sleep.

"I really appreciate your hospitality," Orville told him. "The good food has warmed me up and made me sleepy."

"I hope you get some rest," said Arnold. "We eat breakfast about six o'clock."

When Arnold opened the door to the room, Orville thought there was some mistake. It was a child's room! There was a single bed big enough for an adult to sleep in, but the wallpaper and other furnishings were for a boy.

"I don't want to put your son out," said Orville. "I really don't mind sleeping on the floor."

"You won't put him out," said Arnold. "My son died about this time last year. My wife can't bring herself to change his room or put his things away."

"I'm so sorry!" said Orville. "What happened to him?"

"Timmy had just had his fourth birthday," said Arnold. "Doreen had made him a cake and I had bought him a puppy. We let the puppy stay in his room that night, and I guess sometime in the night the puppy wanted out. Timmy had seen us let him out that afternoon, so he must have thought he could do it, too. It was snowing that night like it is tonight, and the temperature was near zero. We woke to a freezing cold house the next morning. We hurried downstairs and found the front door open. Then we saw the puppy's tracks and Timmy's footprints in the snow. Since they weren't completely covered, we clung to the hope that they hadn't been outside long. Of course, I followed the tracks and they led me to Timmy. He had frozen to death and the puppy was gone. We never found him."

"Oh, Lord!" said Orville. ""How awful!"

"My wife won't accept it," Arnold continued. "She says she actually sees Timmy outside sometimes. She says he comes inside from the cold and tries to get warm. She slept in here for weeks, insisting that he'd get into bed with her at night. She swore she could feel his cold little hands on her back as he snuggled up to her. I finally made her stop sleeping in here. I was afraid she would lose her mind."

"I don't know what to say," said Orville. "That is so tragic!"

Arnold nodded. "I hope you rest well. I'll call you for breakfast."

Orville heard his footsteps go down the hall. Orville went to bed at once. In a few minutes, Doreen's softer steps went by and the house got quiet. For a few minutes, Orville watched the snowfall. The wind wailed when it gusted like a child crying. He pulled the covers tighter and finally fell asleep. Hours passed uneventful.

Then suddenly, Orville awoke to a strange sensation. Something cold was against his back. It was the touch of a small, cold hand. It was colder than anything he had ever imagined. He threw back the covers and looked in the bed. There was absolutely nothing there to have caused the cold. He stood there, not feeling so cocky anymore. He pulled the covers and pillow off the bed and slept the rest of the night on the floor.

The next morning, Orville went to breakfast undecided about whether he should tell them about the experience. He sat shivering as he drank steaming black coffee. Doreen watched him for a short time before she spoke.

"You felt him, didn't you?" she asked.

The question took Orville by surprise.

"Yes," he answered honestly. "How did you know?"

She smiled sadly before she answered. Then she looked first at her husband and then at Orville.

"You're shivering," she said. "You can't control it. After he would touch me, it would be hours before I could feel warm again."

Arnold drove Orville to town after breakfast and helped him replace the broken fan belt.

"Thanks again for your hospitality," said Orville as he drove away. *Though hauntspitality is a better word, he thought.*

Orville lived through the war and told his story for the rest of his life. He said that every time he thought about it, his blood would still run cold.

The Pine Thicket

Ruth Newman came to live on her grandmother's farm after her mother died. It had happened in the spring, so the summer on the farm had been lonely. The Foley children, Anna and Leonard, lived on the next farm, but they were older. They didn't want to play games with Ruth very often, but they loved to tell her stories.

"Don't go into the pine thicket," warned Anna.

Ruth saw the pine thicket every time they went out to the main road to the little country store. They had to go right by it. *That's no big deal,* she thought. *It's just a bunch of trees.*

"What's in the pine thicket?" she asked.

"Old man Black with his walking stick!" said Leonard. "He dresses in black and sits there in the shadows. And he doesn't like children!"

"Why not?" asked Ruth.

"Those woods have been in the Black family for years. Kids leave litter and set fires sometimes. They say the woods are haunted, so the Blacks chase people away. Some kids have gone in there after dark and never been seen again," Leonard told her.

They're just trying to scare me, she thought. *Anyway, Grandmother never lets me go out after dark.*

"I don't think I'll ever run into Mr. Black," she said, but Anna and Leonard just exchanged knowing glances and shook their heads.

Ruth meant to ask her grandmother about the Blacks and the pine thicket, but her grandmother kept her so busy with chores that it slipped her mind. Her grandmother had a knack for having fun even when doing hard work, so Ruth had no reason to dwell on anything sinister.

Then one afternoon, just as the sun was almost out of sight, Ruth's grandmother called to her.

"Ruth, honey, I'm out of oil for the lanterns. I can see how to milk the cows tonight, but I'll need the lanterns in the morning. While I get the milking done, I want you to run to the store for me and get the oil."

The request took Ruth by surprise. It would be dark by the time she got to the store and started back.

"Grandmother, couldn't it wait until morning?" she asked.

"No, I need the oil tonight," Grandmother answered. "You're not afraid to go by yourself, are you?"

"Oh, no!" Ruth answered quickly, taking the money her grandmother held out to her. "I'll hurry right back!"

Ruth hurried down the country lane as her grandmother headed toward the barn. The sun was still not completely gone from sight, but the pine thicket was already filled with dark shadows. Some were menacing and moving! Ruth ran as fast as she could until the pine thicket was far behind her. She stopped to catch her breath and realized what she had seen was probably only the breeze blowing the branches. She laughed at herself.

When Ruth reached the store, it was closed. She walked back to the garden. The owner, Mrs. Myrt, lived in back of the store and could often be found in her garden.

"Mrs. Myrt?" Ruth called.

"Lordy me, you gave me a start!" Mrs. Myrt laughed. "I was just getting me a squash to cook for supper. Here, let me pull one to take to your grandmother."

Ruth didn't want any delays, but she couldn't be rude. She waited while Mrs. Myrt pulled a squash and then stopped to add a few ears of late corn.

"I'll put these in a bag so it will be easy for you to carry," Mrs. Myrt told her. "Now what else can I do for you?"

Ruth purchased the oil and thanked Mrs. Myrt for the squash and corn. Then she hurried away before Mrs. Myrt thought of something else.

It was dusk now, but still there was enough light for her to see. As she rounded a bend in the lane by the pine thicket, she saw something huge in the road. She stopped when she realized the Foley's fighting bull had gotten out again! She had no choice but to slip into the thicket before it saw her. She tried to stay out of sight, but parallel with the lane until she got around the bull. When she figured she had gone past him, she inched over to where she thought the lane was. It wasn't there. She was lost and it was too dark for her to see which way to go. She was close to crying when a voice came from behind her.

"It's okay. I'll walk you home."

Ruth whirled around to see a bent, old man emerge from among the trees. He was dressed in a black suit and carried a walking stick in his right hand. In his left hand, he held a lantern with a strange soft glow. She remembered the Foley kids' warning! This old man didn't seem to hate her, though. In fact, his voice put her at ease.

"The Foley's should do something about that bull. He's going to hurt somebody one of these days."

"I know," Ruth answered. "I was afraid he'd hurt me, so I ran into your woods. I'm afraid I got lost."

"I'll have you home in no time," he said. "Your grandmother will be worried."

"Thank you," Ruth said, following along behind Mr. Black. "Do you know my grandmother?"

"She's always been a good neighbor," he answered.

Soon, Ruth could see the light in her grandmother's window. The bull was no where in sight now.

"You'll be safe now," he said, "so I'll leave you."

"I don't know what I would have done if you hadn't come along," she said.

"I try to keep an eye out for people lost in my woods," he answered. "Some even think the thicket is haunted."

"I'm glad you were there tonight," Ruth told him. "I wouldn't want to tell my grandmother, but I must confess I'm afraid of the dark!"

The old man smiled faintly in the soft glow of the light.

"I know how you feel," he told her. "I felt the same way when I was alive!"

Before Ruth recovered from the shock, the old man, the walking stick, and the soft glowing lantern vanished before her eyes.

The One That Got Away

"This lake has the biggest fish I've ever seen," Byron Ballard said to his Uncle Basil. "I'm sure glad you bought this farm. I hope you'll let me come fish every summer!"

"You are welcome to fish from the bank," said Uncle Basil, "but I don't want you to go out in the boat. There are stories around here that there are things in that lake other than big fish!"

"What kind of things?" asked Byron. "You mean alligators?"

"No," said Uncle Basil. "Strange things."

"What kind of strange things?" Byron asked.

"Spirits of the dead!" his uncle told him.

"Did anybody drown in this lake?" asked Byron.

"Not since I've owned it, but it spooks me a little," said Uncle Basil. "See that patch of fog out there? Even when it's a sunny day, it hovers there like a body floating."

"What causes that?" Byron wanted to know.

"I don't have an answer for that," said Uncle Basil.

"This is a man made lake. The man who owned the farm before me had it dug. He had one breakdown of machinery after another, but he kept digging. The lake is fed by a fresh water stream that used to have a little island in it."

"Did that cause the problems?" asked Byron.

"Maybe it was in a way," Uncle Basil explained. "One of the workers was hurt, and he wouldn't go back to his job. He said he played on the island as a child and found all kinds of arrowheads. There was a story that medicine men performed sacred rituals there. The worker said it was wrong to put a lake over sacred ground. He said the lake was cursed."

"You don't believe in all that, do you, Uncle Basil?" asked Byron.

"I believe there are powers we don't understand," said Uncle Basil, "and I believe there can be dire consequences if we tangle with them. That patch of fog always stays in that place where the island was. I can't explain it, so I don't want you out on the lake taking chances. You stay on the bank. Do you understand?"

"Yes, Uncle Basil," said Byron.

Byron fished from the bank all day. Once he caught a huge fish, only to have it jump off the hook. He didn't want to end up with only a story about *the one that got away*. He wanted a big fish he could have mounted and point out to all his friends. All the prize fish must be in the center of the lake.

He thought about it all through dinner, and he was still thinking about it when he went to bed. *After Uncle Basil goes to sleep, I'll bet I could sneak down to the dock and take the small boat out, and he would never know!* Shortly after midnight when he heard Uncle Basil snoring, he decided to try!

Byron untied the boat and rowed silently across the lake. The water was still and sparkling like silver in the moonlight. Inside the house, Uncle Basil woke from a restless sleep. Something was wrong, but he couldn't put his finger on it. He got up, pulled on his pants, and went to check on Byron. The boy was gone! He couldn't believe he would disobey him and go out on the lake, yet a part of him wasn't surprised. He would probably have been tempted, too, at Byron's age. He ran to the dock, hoping he was wrong.

His small rowboat was missing. He untied his large boat and pushed off. He rowed hard and soon he saw Byron ahead.

"Byron! Come back!" he shouted.

Byron heard him, but now he was nearing the fog-covered center of the lake. The wind picked up and the water swelled in high waves. He looked down and was surprised to see that the water was now a dark green. He was very frightened now. He knew he had done a very foolish thing. He tried to turn back, but the water churned and sent the small boat spinning in a circle at the edge of the fog.

"Stop!" screamed Uncle Basil.

Byron tried! But he screamed and threw down the oars, as a white glowing hand of bones reached out and grabbed the boat. Byron flew into the water.

Uncle Basil was there now, throwing something.
"Catch the line, Byron!" he ordered. "Hold on!"
By some miracle, he did, and Uncle Basil pulled him into his boat just as the smaller boat flew apart and vanished into the fog.
Byron never fished from a boat again. He never worried about catching the big fish. He was just grateful that, with Uncle Basil's help, he was the one that got away!

Searchers

It was one of those days when you don't expect anything to happen. The sweltering weather had finally given way to cool temperatures, and Keith and Theresa Bernard decided to take advantage of it. They decided that a drive in the country and a picnic would be the perfect way to do it. They had gone on far away vacations before, but this year they had decided to search out the quaint spots closer to home.

They were a couple of hours away from town when they saw the perfect shady area off to the side of the road. Keith pulled over, and Theresa soon had the picnic lunch set up. She had expected the shade to be cool, but almost at once, she began to feel unnaturally cold.

"Do you feel chilly?" she asked Keith.

"No, feels great to me," he said. "Are your allergies acting up again?"

Before she could answer, they were interrupted by the sound of footsteps. They looked up to see a young woman walking toward them from among the trees.

"I'm looking for my son," she said, stopping a few feet away from the clearing where they were eating.

"We haven't seen anyone," Keith responded, "but, of course, we just got here s few minutes ago."

"I've got to find him!" she said in a desperate voice.

"Tell us about him," said Theresa. "Maybe we can help you look. How long has he been gone?"

"A while," she answered vaguely.

"Come have some food and tell us what happened," said Keith.

She made no move toward the food. They could see how upset she was, so they made no attempt to interrupt when she started to talk.

"He was in band camp this week," she said. "I was worried because my Billy has allergies and is bothered by the heat."

Theresa nodded, but remained silent. *I can understand the allergies, she thought. I am chilling right now.*

"I was afraid Billy might get sick," the woman continued, "and I was right. The band director called me to come get Billy yesterday. I drove up right away. It's only about 70 miles, you know."

They didn't know, but she paused as if waiting for them to agree about the distance. They nodded and she continued.

"I thought we would get home before dark, but the storms came, you know."

They did know that, so they nodded again.

"Well," she said, "the rain fell so hard, I couldn't see the road. I pulled over just around the bend there to wait until it slacked off. The rain just kept on pouring down and, when the lightning flashed, I saw an old house up there among some trees. The clouds were billowing up so black that I was afraid for us to stay in the car, so I told Billy we had to make a run for it."

She gazed in that direction and Theresa felt shivers run through her body. *This isn't my allergies, she decided. There is something about this place that makes me uneasy.* Theresa looked where the woman was looking, but all she could see were trees.

"Billy hesitated at first," said the woman. "I thought he was just afraid to get out in the storm, but he said, 'Mom, we can't go in there. That's the old Cutter House. It's haunted! Mr. Cutter killed his wife and son there and then hanged himself in the corner of the living room. They told us about it at camp!'"

"That's nonsense," I told him. "That was just a camp tale. There are no such things as ghosts! Come on, now! Hurry! The storm is getting worse! Let's get to that house while we can!'

"I opened the car door and started running. I heard Billy's door open and slam, and I heard his footsteps behind me. Suddenly, I heard a thud and a cry. I whirled around as Billy was getting up. He'd slipped in the mud and skinned his finger, but he ran on after me.

"I don't mind telling you, I was relieved to get inside. The wind whipped the trees and bowed the branches low in submission to its power. We could see the car well enough to see a huge tree fall across the top of the car. I knew then that we wouldn't be going anywhere, even after the storm passed over. I looked around to see how I could make us comfortable for the night.

"There was some old furniture, so we broke it and started a fire in the old fire place so we could dry out. I found a Band-aid in my purse and bandaged Billy's finger.

'I've got some candy in my pocket,' Billy told me. He pulled out two slightly smashed Reese's cups and we ate them for supper. Then we lay down on the floor and listened to the storm until we got sleepy.

"Just as we were drifting off, a THUMP woke us!

'What was that, Mom?' Billy asked sitting up and looking around the room, frightened.

"The wind just blew a limb against the house, I told him. But I wasn't sure. It sounded like the sound came from inside the house. The firelight cast strange shadows in the dusty old room.

"Let's try to get some sleep, I told him. We'll walk over to a neighbor's house in the morning and get some help. The storm will be over by then.

"It did die down for a while, and we were able to sleep. Then it started up again, this time worse than ever! The fire had gone out and the room was in total darkness. Billy moved close to me and said, 'Hold my hand, Mom.' I took his hand and still felt the Band-aid on his finger.

"Somehow we managed to sleep. I was so tired, I barely heard Billy cry out when the thunder boomed and the wind banged limbs against the house.

"When I woke, the storm was over. Sunlight was shining through the window. I was still holding Billy's hand, and I looked down to see if he was still asleep.

"That's when I saw it. I was holding **just** his hand. It had been cut away! There was a pool of blood, but the rest of him was gone! I was too shocked to scream or move. I sat staring horrified as a wispy, mist figure with an axe floated toward me from the corner!"

Keith and Theresa were on the verge of shock themselves. The woman was surely crazy, but she seemed so sincere. Goosebumps covered Theresa's arms.

"My God!" she said. "How did you get away from it?"

The woman looked at them with an odd smile. Slowly, she answered the question.

"I didn't!"

With that, she vanished into thin air before their eyes.

Of course, they looked for her. They couldn't believe they had been talking to a ghost! But there was not a trace of her among the trees. They snatched up the remains of their picnic lunch and hurried to their car. They drove around the bend and stared in disbelief at a tumbled down old house among the trees. The wind picked up and began to howl, even though it was still a picture perfect day. Keith and Theresa drove away as fast as they could and never looked back.

But out there somewhere is a boy searching for his hand, a mother searching for her son, and an evil ghost with an axe searching for another victim.

Wings

Clyde Creighton loved everything with wings. The mystery of flight left him in awe and wonder. He spent every minute he could watching airplanes, birds, and butterflies.

"I'm going to fly like that someday," he'd tell his parents. "I'm going to learn how they do it!"

They would smile at Clyde, but inside they felt sad to hear him say that. They knew he would never be able to learn much about things with wings, because Clyde wasn't the smartest little boy in the world. A birth defect had limited his power to learn.

Clyde watched the other children go by on their way to school, and he dreamed of the day he could go with them. You had to be six, and he was only five now. He sometimes watched the children chasing butterflies and heard them talking about science projects they were doing at school. He didn't understand what that meant, but he knew it must be fun to learn about things that could fly.

Even though Clyde didn't know about these things, they seemed to know about him. Birds would sit on his shoulders, butterflies would light in his hand, and bees would buzz around his face without stinging him. His father had actually seen the pilots of small planes dip their wings at Clyde when he was playing outside as they flew over.

"I want to fly!" Clyde would say. "Will it be long?"

"Maybe not too long," his mother would tell him.

Fred and Althea Creighton would look at their son and then at each other. Fred would start to speak to the boy about his situation, but Althea would shake her head. Fred's shoulders would slump and he'd turn away.

Clyde never noticed because he was always too busy watching the sky.

Every night at bedtime, there was sure to be a disagreement between Fred and Althea.

"You can't protect him forever," Fred would argue. "He needs a special school. It would be better if we put him there now."

"No!" Althea would insist. "Public schools have programs for special needs children now. He needs to be here in his own home with us!"

"You spoil him too much," Fred would tell her. "He'll never learn to be independent unless you stop babying him."

"I don't baby him," Althea would protest.

"Yes, you do!" Fred would insist. "You still let him sleep on that old feather pillow that he's had since he was born! You need to get rid of that thing and get something new."

"Be a little patient with him, Fred," Althea would plead. "He can't sleep without his feather pillow."

"How do you know?" Fred would ask. "He's never tried!"

"He's just a little boy," Althea would say. "His pillow is like a security blanket. Lots of kids have things like that. He'll give it up when he's ready."

"And when will that be?" Fred would ask. "When he's forty? He will never give up childish things on his own, Althea, because he'll always think like a child! Why can't you accept that?"

"Why can't you?" Althea would cry. "You can't face the fact that the brilliant Fred Creighton has a mentally handicapped son! You can't send him away and expect him to be like everybody else. He's different!"

"I know he's different, Althea," Fred would say, a little more calmly. "I love him and I'm not ashamed of him. I just think he can learn to do more things for himself if he is away from us. You do everything for him. And you let him fill his head with all this nonsense about flying. You are encouraging him to do the impossible, and he'll end up hurt and disappointed."

When Clyde would hear the loud voices of his parents coming from the next room, he would lie there frightened and try to shut them out. He couldn't understand what they were saying, but he knew they were unhappy about him. He would pull his feather pillow around his ears until the house got quiet.

As Clyde would drift off to sleep, he'd hear the soft whirring of wings, and the feathers in his pillow would settle around him protectively. Sometimes he felt like he had wings of his own. The next morning, Clyde would have forgotten about the night before and be full of questions again.

"How do things fly?" he'd ask his father.

"It's too hard for a little boy your age to understand," Fred would tell him. "You have to know about things like lift, drag, thrust, gravity, air currents, and things like that."

Clyde would be silent until his father left for work. Then he would ask his mother the same question.

"I don't know," she said one day. "How do you think things fly, Clyde?"

"I think the Wing Spirit helps them," he answered without hesitation.

"What makes you think that?" she asked him.

"The Wing Spirit said so," Clyde replied.

"Tell me about the Wing Spirit," said Althea.

"It's my friend," said Clyde. "It lives in my pillow and it talks to me at night."

"What does it look like?" asked Althea.

"I can't see it yet," Clyde explained. "It says I can see it when we fly away sometime."

Althea wondered if he had heard her and Fred talking about sending him away. Maybe he had invented the Wing Spirit because he was afraid. If Fred heard him talking like this, he'd probably do something drastic right away.

"Let's let the Wing Spirit be our secret for a while," she told Clyde.

"Okay," said the boy. "Daddy might not like him anyway."

She hugged her son and sent him off to play, but she noticed he left his toys and sat near the birdbath watching the birds.

Things were quiet in the Creighton household for several days after that. Althea was relieved that Fred said nothing more about sending Clyde away. She knew they would have to make a decision soon, though, because Clyde's sixth birthday was approaching.

Althea wanted this birthday to be special for Clyde, so she was especially surprised and happy when Fred suggested the perfect gift.

"Let's hire a pilot to take Clyde flying," he said. "It doesn't take much money to hire a little Cessna for an hour or so. I think our budget can stand it."

Althea threw her arms around her husband and kissed him.

"He'll be so happy!" she said.

They told Clyde together. Althea knew she would never forget the look of joy on her son's face when he heard the news.

"I'm going to fly on my birthday!" he said over and over.

When Clyde woke up on his birthday, rain was pounding against his bedroom windows and lightning was bolting across the sky. It meant nothing to Clyde. He got out of bed and dressed to go flying.

"We can't fly in thunderstorms," explained his father. "It would be very dangerous."

"Birds do it," said Clyde. "They don't get hurt."

"That's different," said Fred. "They were born to fly."

"I was, too," said Clyde. "I'm going to fly today on my birthday."

For most of the day, Clyde sat by the window and looked at the heavy-clouded sky. Althea could hardly coax him away to eat his birthday cake.

At bedtime, Fred carried Clyde up to bed and listened to his prayers before tucking him in. Clyde forgot that he wasn't supposed to mention the Wing Spirit to his father.

"Please, Wing Spirit! Let me fly on my birthday," he prayed.

"Wing Spirit?" he asked. "A Wing Spirit won't answer your prayers. I'm tired of all this nonsense, Clyde. Now be quiet and go to sleep."

His stern voice upset Clyde, and he began to sob into his pillow.

"Give me that silly pillow," said Fred, reaching to take it from under Clyde's head.

"No!" screamed the boy, holding tightly to the pillow. "No! I want to be with the Wing Spirit!"

Fred tugged at the pillow, but Clyde held on.

"Fred, please!" said Althea from the doorway. "Leave him alone. Can't you see how upset he is? You are only making it worse by taking his pillow."

Fred stopped pulling and Clyde jerked the pillow away. Fred walked to their room and motioned for Althea to follow.

"What is all this about a Winged Spirit?" Fred demanded to know.

"It's just one of those imaginary friends that children have at this age," said Althea.

"This is the last straw," Fred told her. "This is the last night he is sleeping with that pillow. I'm throwing it away myself tomorrow. Then we are going to start looking for a suitable school."

In the next room, Clyde heard what they were saying and he continued to cry. He pulled the pillow around his ears to stop their voices. The Wing Spirit began to speak to him softly. Clyde listened and stopped crying. Then he smiled.

Althea and Fred went to bed without settling the argument. Sometime in the night, Althea woke to a flapping sound going by her window. She thought she heard Clyde call out her name, but when she didn't hear it again, she decided it must have been the wind. She turned over and went back to sleep.

Morning brought sunshine streaming through the windows. Fred felt badly that he had yelled at Clyde. Today he would take him to the airport for his flight. He went to wake his son and tell him the news.

"Oh, my God!"

Althea heard his anguished cry from the doorway. She ran to the room where Fred stood sobbing. She saw her son's still, cold body on the bed. Beside him, the pillow was ripped open and every single feather was gone!

Horse Calls

Abigail Alley heard the shots down in the woods by the pasture about an hour before she heard the knocking on her door.

It must be Carey and Claude Franklin out hunting again, she thought. *Their father shouldn't let them out with guns. Neither one of them has a lick of sense when it comes to shooting. They'll fire at anything that moves.*

Sensible people knew it was not a good night for hunting. The wind was picking up and the clouds were boiling up in the west, threatening rain. Not much would be moving tonight.

She had herded Old John into the stable earlier and fed him, even though the stubborn old mule had resisted all the way. She'd have to call up Sam, the big black horse that she teamed with Old John when she wanted to pull the heavy wagon. Sam had a calming effect on Old John. Sam usually came up by himself when a storm was coming, but he hadn't come up yet tonight.

She was relieved when she heard no more shooting. It wasn't safe to be outside when Carey and Claude were on the prowl.

They must have gone home for supper, she thought. *I'd better go look for Sam while it's safe!*

She had reached the door when she heard the knocking. It was her neighbor, Hollis Neville.

"Momma's got the flu," he said. "She sent me to see if you could come over and help her."

"Of course, Hollis," she told him. "Hurry back home before the storm hits. Tell her I'll be there as soon as I can."

She watched the boy mount his horse and ride toward home. She looked at the threatening sky and made a decision. She wouldn't have time to go look for Sam and take the heavy wagon. She would have to hitch Old John to the buggy and leave right away in order to beat the storm. It was too bad she couldn't take Sam. Hollis loved that horse. But it might be better to take the buggy tonight with the rain coming in. The heavy wagon might bog down in the muddy road.

Abigail worried a little when she saw Sam's stall empty. She would leave the barn door open so he could come inside out of the rain. As she opened Old John's stall door, she hoped he wouldn't have one of his stubborn spells. He didn't like the rain very much. When he'd have one of his stubborn spells, he would take the first opportunity to break loose and run back home.

Old John flicked one ear when Abigail put the bridle on him to lead him out. As she hitched him to the buggy, he pawed the ground once with his right front foot, but, other than that, he offered no resistance.

Abigail took down a bag of herbs from the barn wall and placed them on the buggy seat. Then she climbed in, pulled on the reins, and held tightly as the buggy lurched forward.

"Easy, John," she said, as thunder rumbled along the ridge ahead where she was going. Large, cold raindrops began to sting against her face now and then, as if warning of things to come. She was glad she had brought her lantern because the dark was coming very fast.

As they made the turn at the bend in the road, Abigail's gaze fell on something in the ditch. She pulled the reins for Old John to stop. He looked around and gave his head a shake to show he wasn't pleased, but he obeyed.

Abigail leaned over as far as she could from her seat. She held her lantern in her left hand and the reins in her right. Her light shown on a small figure lying very still in the ditch. It was Hollis Neville! His horse must have been spooked by the thunder and thrown him. She hung the lantern on the buggy and, holding the reins tightly, she carefully climbed down. The boy was knocked out, but she couldn't tell how badly he was hurt. She tried to reach him, but she couldn't get close unless she turned loose of Old John's reins.

She hesitated briefly, trying to decide the best course of action. If she climbed back in the buggy and left the boy in the ditch while she went for help, he might get wet and get the flu or pneumonia. If she turned loose of the reins, Old John might quite possibly run away and leave her stranded along with the boy.

She made a quick decision. She couldn't leave the boy.

"John," she said, looking him in the face. "You've got to help me. You can't run!"

Slowly she dropped the reins. Old John moved the buggy slightly forward.

"Steady, John," she coaxed. "Stand still!"

Abigail reached under the boy and lifted him in her arms. As she stepped toward the buggy, Old John laid back his ears in a pose that was all too familiar. She knew he was going to run!

Just as he moved forward, something black filled the narrow road. Old John reared and stopped! Abigail dashed to the buggy, placed Hollis on the seat, and grabbed the reins. She squinted into the darkness and saw that the black thing in the road was Sam! He must have seen her leave and followed the buggy. *But how, she wondered, did he get out of the pasture?* She hadn't brought an extra bridle, so she hoped he'd keep following her. Right now, she had to get Hollis home and into a good, warm bed.

She covered the remaining distance quickly and tied Old John securely to the gate. She hurried inside carrying the boy, and soon she was brewing tea that would break the fever of all the family members. By mid morning, everyone had improved.

Abigail was getting ready to head back home, when Mr. Franklin knocked at the door. Carey and Claude were behind him.

"My boys have something to tell you," he said.

The boys looked at the ground.

"Go on! Tell her what you did!"

"We accidently killed your horse. Sam." said Carey.

"We were scared, so we buried him in your pasture," Claude added.

"What?" exclaimed Abigail. "That's impossible!"

"I'm afraid it's true, Miss Abigail," said Mr. Franklin. "I'm terribly sorry. We've come to pay for the horse."

"But I saw Sam last night on the way over here," said Abigail.

"You couldn't have," said Mr. Franklin. "The boys shot him before the storm hit. I've taken their guns. They won't have them again."

"But he helped me save Hollis. He kept John from running off with the buggy," insisted Abigail.

"Maybe it was another horse," suggested Mr. Franklin. "Let me know what I owe you and I'll see that you're paid."

He and the boys turned and left. Tears were stinging Abigail's eyes, but she blinked them back. There had to be some mistake. She untied John and headed home.

Once she had turned him out to pasture, she walked until she found Sam's grave. There were broken blades of grass leading from the grave to the road and back again. She looked closely at the sod covering the grave. There were four visible hoof prints! Some how he had gone with her to make that one last call.

Crawl Space

Davy Conners wanted somebody to play with. It was hard being an only child, and he had not had time to make new friends since his family had just moved to this new place during the summer. He was encouraged by one thing, though. A new school was being built at the end of his street, and he would be going there in the fall. He would find somebody to play with then, but for now, he had to entertain himself.

He took his blue, hard rubber ball from the shelf in his closet and called to his mother that he was going outside to play. His best friend had given him the ball when he moved away. He had written *To Davy from Randy* on the ball and it had become his favorite toy.

"Keep away from those construction workers," his mother called. "They don't need you underfoot."

Davy pretended he didn't hear her and hurried down the street to the school. Every day he'd watch the workers come and go. Sometimes they would smile and wave at him, but usually they had earphones on, listening to music. He'd wait until they were all gone, and then he would throw his blue ball against the outer wall of the school and catch it when it bounced back.

"You are going to break a window," warned his father, "and then you'll have to pay for it out of your allowance!"

Davy was sure that would never happen. He was a good pitcher and catcher! He ignored his father and kept playing with his ball.

Ker-thump! Pow! Ker-thump! Pow! From the wall to his glove. Over and Over! **Ker-thump! Pow!**

It was getting late and Davy knew his mother would have dinner ready soon. He knew he should go on home, but he decided to toss the ball one more time. His attention was on the ball and he didn't see the rock in front of him. He stumped his toe just as he released the ball. He knew he was off target!

Ker thump! Crash-h-h-h!

He heard glass falling from the window. He couldn't believe this had happened!

I've had it now, he thought! I'll have to pay for that window and I won't have anything left of my allowance. I'll be in trouble at school before I even start!

The only thing to do was to go inside and get the ball. When his friend wrote his name on the ball, he had used permanent ink. Everyone would know it was his.

He moved quickly to the broken window and looked inside. His ball had rolled near an opening in the wall that the construction workers hadn't finished yet. He found a stick and knocked out the remaining jagged glass in the window. Then he crawled through and ran for his ball.

Davy didn't judge his distance well in his eagerness to reach the ball. As he approached, his foot hit the ball, knocking it through the opening in the wall. He knelt down and looked inside. There was a crawl space big enough to get into.

Davy eased himself through the opening. The light was dim and his blue ball did not show up well. He felt around for it. When his hand touched the ball, it rolled farther back in the crawl space. Davy followed until he grasped the ball in his hand. He started to move back, but his tee shirt caught on a nail. While trying to untangle himself, he heard someone coming.

Oh, no! he thought. One of the construction workers must still be here. I'll have to be quiet until he leaves and then crawl out.

Davy stayed still, but he did not hear footsteps going away. Instead, there was a sound Davy didn't recognize at first. **Plop! Scrape!** Then the dim light went out completely. This couldn't be happening! The construction worker was closing up the opening in the wall!

Davy began to scream!

"Wait! Help! Let me out!"

But the sounds continued.

"Help! Please let me out!"

No response came from outside the wall.

Then Davy remembered. The construction workers often wore earphones and listened to music while they worked. The man couldn't hear him! Davy beat on the wall, but the construction worker had finished his job and left the building! Nobody knew that Davy was walled up in the crawl space.

Search parties covered the surrounding area, but there was no sign of Davy. When they saw the broken window, they thought maybe Davy had done it and run away. Finally, they stopped looking.

When school started in the fall, students complained of noises in the wall in the room where the window had been broken.

Ker-thump! Pow!

But nobody believed them.

Students would hear the noise, look over their shoulders, and pull their chairs away. They were afraid that whatever was in the wall might someday come **crash-h-hing** through!

Family Recipe

"These are the strangest snowflakes I've ever seen," said Katrina. "They look big and fluffy, but they sound hard like sleet pelting the window!"

"There's probably some sleet mixed in," replied her grandmother, shifting uncomfortably in her rocking chair by the fire. "The weather here in the mountains is not like your city weather. Why don't you come away from the window and finish your soup while it's hot?"

Even though it sounded more like an order instead of a question, Katrina ignored her grandmother and kept her face pressed against the windowpane. A noise had brought her to the window. She had heard a cry in the storm and thought maybe it was an animal. Now through the swirling white, she could see several forms moving by the old shed. They looked like children playing in the snow, but that was odd because her grandmother had no neighbors for miles around. The children seemed to be looking toward the window, so she raised her hand and waved.

"What are you doing, Katrina?" her grandmother asked.

"Waving at the children," Katrina answered.

"Children?" said the old woman, with a strange edge to her voice. "There are no children around here. Come away from the window!"

"But I see them!" Katrina insisted.

"Your eyes were playing tricks on you!" said the old woman sharply. "Now come finish your soup! There will be no food wasted in this house."

Katrina dutifully returned to the table and swallowed the last bit of soup in the bowl. There was an odd, unpleasant aftertaste. She gulped her tea to take the taste away.

"What kind of soup is this, Grandmother?" she asked, frowning.

"It's a family recipe," the old woman replied. "I use a special ingredient that I store in the old shed. My mother used it, and her mother before her. I had hoped to pass it on, but your mother ran away before I could. Maybe I'll pass it on to you one day."

"Thank you, anyway," said Katrina, "but I don't like it very much."

Ungrateful child, thought the old woman! Just like her mother!

"Your mother wouldn't eat anything to give her strength. That's why she died having you!" said the grandmother.

Katrina felt the longing creeping in again. She wished she had known her mother, but all she had was a picture of a woman with long red hair in a wedding dress. What her grandmother was saying was not at all what her father said. He'd always told her that her mother was the strongest woman he had ever known.

"What was she like when she was my age?" asked Katrina.

The grandmother's eyes glittered as she answered.

"She was an ungrateful child. Always questioning everything, especially the old ways. You remind me of her."

"I'm sorry, Grandmother," Katrina said quickly. "I didn't mean to sound ungrateful. I'm just picky about my food."

"Hummph," grunted the old woman. "Come help me wash the dishes."

There weren't many to wash, so they were done quickly and in silence. The old woman poked up the fire and sat in her rocking chair in front of the fireplace. Her mind seemed far away.

"May I go to my room and read, Grandmother?" asked Katrina. She didn't want to stay there and make her grandmother angry with more unwanted questions.

The old woman nodded, and Katrina hurried toward her room without another word. Actually the old woman was relieved at the girl's request. She welcomed being alone.

As soon as she heard the door close behind Katrina, she made her way to the window as quickly and quietly as possible. Her hand shook as she pulled back the curtain and looked outside. The space around the shed was empty. Of course, she, of all people, knew it had to be. The children couldn't come back. Yet Katrina's insisting that she had seen them had unnerved the old woman greatly. With hands that still shook, she made herself a cup of tea and sipped it before the fire.

I should never have allowed this visit, she thought. *When her father said he had business nearby and wanted Katrina to meet me, I should have refused.*

In her room Katrina looked out the window again. The children were there now, playing in the snow. They motioned for her to come to the shed!

Katrina opened her window and leaned out. A blast of icy air nearly took her breath away. She wondered how the children could play out in the cold so long. It must be because they were used to the climate.

The children moved closer. They were chanting something that Katrina couldn't quite understand. It sounded like *Bone meal! Bone meal! Run! Run! Run!* Katrina thought it must be a game. The air turned into a swirling white cloud, and when the wind died down, the children had vanished. Katrina stood shivering and staring at the empty space beside the shed.

"Katrina!" said a loud voice behind her. "Close that window at once! You will be ill!"

Katina quickly closed it and turned to face her grandmother. The old woman was glaring angrily from the doorway.

"I'm sorry, Grandmother!" said Katrina, but the old woman didn't seem to notice.

"Get to bed at once!" she ordered. "I want no more trouble from you!"

Katrina quickly got into bed and pulled up the covers. The old woman turned and stomped off to her room. After a few minutes, the house was quiet.

Thank goodness Father is coming to get me tomorrow, thought Katrina. *No wonder my mother ran away from here. It's obvious Grandmother doesn't like children.*

Katrina couldn't sleep. She decided to put on her warmest clothes and sneak out to the shed. She was curious about the secret ingredient stored there. Maybe that's where the children went to get warm. She managed to get out without waking her Grandmother.

Katrina reached the shed and tried the door. It was locked. She walked around back and saw a window. She peeked inside. As her eyes adjusted to the dark, she saw an eerie glow from piles of something on the floor. Suddenly, she knew what she was seeing. Piles of human bones! Small bones! The bones of children! They were even near the grinder in the corner. Katrina began to sob!

"So you couldn't leave it alone?" sneered a voice behind her. "You just had to know, so now you can join them!"

As the old woman stepped forward, Katrina could see that she carried a sharp kitchen knife.

"You can't kill me!" cried Katrina. "My father is coming tomorrow!"

"I'll tell him you got homesick and ran away!" said the old woman.

"He wouldn't believe you!" said Katrina.

"I'll take my chances!" the old woman laughed gleefully! She stepped closer to Katrina with the knife.

Suddenly several things happened together. The bones flew through the window and beat at the head of the old woman. The ground bones beat against her face. *Oh, Lord! That's what I thought were snowflakes!* thought Katrina. The old woman threw up her hands to ward off the blows. A white figure with long red hair materialized in front of Katrina. She pointed down the road and vanished. *There's a church down the road, she remembered. Her father said her mother had hidden there when she ran away.* Katrina ran as fast as her legs would go.

The old woman had no time to worry about the girl now. She had a head start anyway and would probably escape like her mother had done years ago. It didn't matter.

There were more of her kind to deal with the innocent ones like Katrina.

Her father will probably send the sheriff, she thought as she made her way back inside. I will wait until the bones settle down and I'll grind them into powder for soup. Let them come and search. They won't find anything but jars of powder for the family recipe!

Hearing Loss

Don and his friend Roy squirmed in their seats at the back of the school auditorium. They saw their new teacher, Mr. Jackson, eyeing them from the door.

"Why does he make us come to these concerts?" asked Don. "They're so boring! None of these amateurs can sing."

"I don't know," replied Roy. "He says the music classes should have a chance to show off their talents to the whole student body."

"What talent?" snickered Don! "They're tone deaf and they are so loud, they are making me deaf, too! How long is the program today?"

"Just an hour," said Roy.

"An hour?" said Don. "I can't take it!"

"You don't have a choice," said Roy, nodding toward the door. "Mr. Jackson is watching."

"I do have a choice," said Don. "At the end of the next song, I'm going to leave. Everybody will be clapping and nobody will notice me."

"Mr. Jackson will," said Roy. "He'll say you're rude. No telling what the punishment will be!"

"I don't care," said Don. "I'm going!"

Neither boy said anything else until the song ended. Then Don stood up and made his way to the door where Mr. Jackson was standing.

As Don approached the door, Mr. Jackson blocked his way.

"Where do you think you're going?" asked Mr. Jackson.

"I'm leaving," said Don.

"Why?" asked Mr. Jackson. "Don't you feel well?"

"No," said Don. "I'm sick! I'm sick and tired of listening to these people who can't sing! I'd rather be playing basketball."

"A little culture won't hurt you," said Mr. Jackson. "Now go back to your seat."

Don looked around and saw Roy watching. He'd never hear the end of it if he went back and sat down.

"I'm leaving!" Don announced defiantly. "I've heard all I want to hear!"

"You're certain?" Mr. Jackson asked.

"I said I don't want to hear any more!" Don told him.

"Very well!" said Mr. Jackson. "Suit yourself!"

With that, he ripped Don's ears off and threw them out the window!

Of course, Don didn't have to listen anymore concerts and there were no more discipline problems at that school.

Some students say that there is one annoying thing now about the concerts. While they are listening to the music, they'll feel a tug on their ear lobes. They know it's that poor boy looking for his ears!

Printed in the United States
42556LVS00002B/1-24